NOTES
FROM THE
DOG

ALSO BY GARY PAULSEN

Alida's Song

The Amazing Life of Birds

The Beet Fields

The Boy Who Owned the School

The Brian Books: *The River, Brian's Winter, Brian's Return,* and *Brian's Hunt*

Canyons

Caught by the Sea: My Life on Boats

The Cookcamp

The Crossing

Danger on Midnight River

Dogsong

Father Water, Mother Woods

The Glass Café

Guts: The True Stories Behind Hatchet *and the Brian Books*

Harris and Me

Hatchet

The Haymeadow

How Angel Peterson Got His Name

The Island

Lawn Boy

The Legend of Bass Reeves

Molly McGinty Has a Really Good Day

The Monument

Mudshark

My Life in Dog Years

Nightjohn

The Night the White Deer Died

Puppies, Dogs, and Blue Northers

The Quilt

The Rifle

Sarny: A Life Remembered

The Schernoff Discoveries

Soldier's Heart

The Time Hackers

The Transall Saga

Tucket's Travels (the Tucket's West series, Books One through Five)

The Voyage of the Frog

The White Fox Chronicles

The Winter Room

Picture books, illustrated by Ruth Wright Paulsen:

Canoe Days and *Dogteam*

NOTES
FROM THE
DOG

GARY PAULSEN

WENDY
LAMB
BOOKS

Copyright © 2009 by Gary Paulsen

All rights reserved.
Published in the United States by Wendy Lamb Books,
an imprint of Random House Children's Books,
a division of Random House, Inc., New York.

Wendy Lamb Books and the colophon are trademarks
of Random House, Inc.

Visit us on the Web! www.randomhouse.com/teens
Educators and librarians, for a variety of teaching tools,
visit us at www.randomhouse.com/teachers

Library of Congress Cataloging-in-Publication Data
Paulsen, Gary.
Notes from the dog / Gary Paulsen. — 1st ed.
p. cm.
Summary: When Johanna shows up at the beginning of summer to house sit
next door to Finn, he has no idea of the profound effect she will have
on his life by the time summer vacation is over.
ISBN: 978-0-385-73845-3 (trade)—ISBN: 978-0-385-90730-9 (lib. bdg.)
ISBN: 978-0-375-89450-3 (e-book)
[1. Cancer—Fiction. 2. Neighbors—Fiction. 3. Self-confidence—Fiction.
4. Gardening—Fiction.] I. Title.
PZ7.P2843No 2009   [Fic]—dc22   2009013300

Printed in the United States of America
10 9 8 7 6 5 4 3 2 1
First Edition

*This book is dedicated with all respect and hope
to everyone who has ever faced cancer.*

To every thing there is a season,
a time for every purpose under the sun.
A time to be born,
and a time to die.
A time to plant,
and a time to reap.

A time to weep,
and a time to laugh.
A time to mourn,
and a time to dance.

—ECCLESIASTES 3

1

Sometimes having company is not all it's cracked up to be.

I was sitting on the front steps of my house with Matthew and Dylan. Matthew was listening to his ear buds, eyes closed, half-humming, half-singing the good parts of the song like he always does, and Dylan was asleep on the ground, snoring and twitching. Matthew's into his music and Dylan's a dog so I didn't pay much attention to either of them. I was trying to read.

Matthew's the only true friend I've got.

He's not my best friend. That's Carl, because we've always got a lot of the same classes and spend the most time together in school. Matthew's not even my oldest friend. That's Jamie, because I've known her since we went to nursery school together. He's definitely not my most fun friend—that would have to be Christopher, who goes to a school for the gifted and always has some crazy story to tell about the supersmart people he knows.

Matthew lives right across the street and is always over at my house. That summer, he was actually living with us, because his parents were in the middle of a divorce. Their house was for sale and they'd each recently moved into nearby apartments. But Matthew had said he wasn't going to learn how to do the shared custody thing on his summer vacation. Then he'd said he'd just stay with us until everything got settled. I was impressed that Matthew called the shots that way, but not surprised that his folks and my dad agreed; Matthew has a way of always making sense so people go along with him.

But that's not what makes him my true friend. It's because he's the only person I know who doesn't make me feel like he's drifted off in his head when I'm talking. Anyone who listens to everything you have to say, even the bad stuff and the boring things that don't interest them, is a true friend. Matthew's always been the only person who's easy for me to talk to. He's a lot like Dylan when you think about it.

Matthew and I aren't anything alike. I know, for instance, that it's got to be easier to be Matthew than it is to be me. There's something so . . . easy about the way he does everything. He gets better grades than me, even though he hardly ever studies. He's on about a million teams at school, and whatever he does in football, baseball, basketball, tennis or track, he looks confident in a way that I never do.

He has friends in every group at school: the brainy people, who, even in middle school, are starting to worry about the "com app" (that's the universal college application form, but I only know that because I Googled the word after I heard them talking about it so much); the jocks, who carpool to their orthopedic doctor appointments together and brag about torn cartilage and bad sprains; the theater and band and orchestra members, who call themselves the arty geeks and then laugh, like it's some big joke on everyone else; and, of course, the losers.

Like me.

Matthew would never call me a loser, not to my face and not behind my back, either, but we both know that I don't fit in and that I'm just biding my time in middle school, waiting for high school and then college, after which I hope I can get a job where I'll be able to work by myself.

It's not that I don't like people, but they make me uncomfortable. I feel like an alien dropped onto a strange planet and that I always have to be on the lookout for clues and cues on how to act and what to say. It's exhausting to always feel like you don't belong anywhere and then worry that you're going to say the wrong thing all the time.

Real people seem so . . . mysterious and, I don't

know, high-maintenance to me. People in books, though, I like them just fine. I read a lot, partly because when I was little and my dad couldn't afford sitters, he'd drag me to the library for his study groups. He was in night school and he's been there ever since. He'd sit me at a table near him and his classmates and give me a pile of books, a bag of pretzels and some juice boxes.

"I wish I had a dollar for every hour I've spent in the library," he always says. I have to agree—we'd probably never have to worry about money again.

So now I don't feel normal unless I've got a book in my hands, and I feel the most normal when I'm lost in a story and can ignore the complicated situations around me that never seem to work out as neatly as they do in books.

So, on that day, Matthew and Dylan and I were sitting in front of my house. It was a week after school let out for the summer.

A completely bald woman drove up, parked in front of the house next door and jumped out of her car.

I knew she'd moved in a couple of weeks ago to house-sit for our neighbors, professors on sabbatical. I'd seen her a few times from my kitchen window, but I hadn't spoken to her. I hadn't noticed she was bald, either, and that kind of detail didn't seem like one I'd miss.

She was probably in her early twenties. She was wearing faded jeans that looked way too big for her and purple cowboy boots. She carried a leather backpack and had one of those bumpy fisherman sweaters draped over her shoulders even though it was hot.

She saw me, waved and headed in our direction.

Dylan sat up as she got closer and looked at her with that teeth-baring border collie grin that scares people who don't know that dogs can smile. I kicked Matthew. He opened his eyes and, when he saw that we had company, took his ear buds out. I sat up straight and sucked in my gut, trying to look tall and thin. A guy can dream.

The woman made a beeline for Dylan and shook his paw. "Hello, dog." Only then did she speak to us, one hand on Dylan, who leaned against her thigh. "In this world, you either like dogs or you don't, and I don't understand the ones who don't, so I'm glad to finally meet the three of you."

I felt guilty the way she said "finally." Maybe I should have gone over and introduced myself. Do good neighbors bring cookies or something when new people move in? I wouldn't know, everyone seems to have lived on my block forever, like prehistoric flies stuck in amber.

"Well, no . . . uh . . . we haven't met, but I've . . . uh . . . seen you before . . . at least I think it was you," I mumbled, trying not to glance at her head.

"Oh, right." She dug in her backpack, pulled out a wad of red hair, shook it and smoothed it down. "I usually wear my wig, but I took it off in the car to feel the fresh air on my head."

"Have you always been bald?" Matthew asked like it was a perfectly normal question.

I would never have said anything about her being bald. One time Jamie cried for three straight hours when a "trim" turned out to be something she called "a five-inch hack" so I figure hair is a tricky subject with girls and not one you bring up if you can avoid it. My father says it's good manners to avoid discussing sex, religion, politics and money in social situations. I think you should add hair to that list.

Actually, it's a good idea to avoid discussing *anything* in social situations. A better idea is to avoid social situations in general.

"Oh, no," she said to Matthew. "I lost my hair during chemo."

We must have flinched. She said, more gently, "My name is Johanna Jackson and I'm a breast cancer survivor." Up close I could see that she had green eyes and freckles all over her face. She never stopped smiling as she looked from me to Matthew to Dylan, who was now lying on his back, paws in the air, begging her to scratch his chest.

"I'm Matthew, this is Finn and that's Dylan. How long have you been cured?" Matthew didn't miss a beat.

"Well, I don't know that you're ever *cured*." She

found the tickle spot on Dylan's ribs that makes his back legs start pedaling with that doggy bliss thing that always makes me wonder what it would feel like. Just to lie there while somebody rubs your belly, with a back leg twitching . . .

"Then how can you call yourself a survivor?" All of a sudden, Matthew was an unlimited source of awkward questions.

"In my book, if you live one split second after hearing news like that, you're a survivor." Johanna finally looked away from Dylan and back up at us.

"Is your hair going to come back?" I couldn't believe I was the one who asked that.

"The doctors say yes, and maybe even different than it was before. I'm hoping for straight blond hair the next time around. You know, give the California beach babe look a whirl."

Right now Johanna was the skinniest, palest thing I'd ever seen. I didn't think "babe" was a look she was going to pull off.

"I don't know." Matthew studied her carefully. "Why go back to all that washing and combing? Besides, you have a nice skull."

Johanna laughed. "Now, there's something you don't hear every day. Dylan as in Dylan Thomas or Dylan as in Bob Dylan?" She turned to me and changed the subject smoothly. I wished I could do that.

"The songwriter. My dad thinks Bob Dylan is"—

7

and here I repeated the words I'd heard him say a million times—"a cultural icon, and that the socio-political meaning and impact of the music is more than worthy subject matter for his master's thesis." I paused, saw her nod and then went for it. "Johanna—as in 'Visions of Johanna'?"

She beamed at me. "Dog people *and* Dylan fans. I've come to the right place."

I shrugged, trying not to look pleased. She got it!

"Would you both sign my book?" Johanna pulled a tattered notebook from her backpack and handed it to Matthew. He scrawled his name and handed it to me.

"Okay," I said, "but . . . um . . . why?"

"Because every day in my journal I write down the best thing that's happened to me. Today it's you."

When Johanna said that, I felt light, warm in that spot just above my stomach where it usually feels clenched and tight.

2

 Before Johanna, I had never been the highlight of anyone's day.

The morning after meeting her I was back on the front steps of our house, eating breakfast. My dad had left for work and Matthew had headed out with some guys from school, so I was alone. Except for Dylan, of course.

Dad works as a bookkeeper for a neighborhood clinic, and he's been in school part-time for as long as I can remember. First he went back to get his bachelor's degree and now he's working on his master's. He's hardly ever home. And when he is, he looks a little surprised when I speak to him, as if he hadn't realized I was in the room. We get along fine, but I've never once gotten the feeling that I'm the best part of *his* day.

My mother "pulled up stakes" when I was a baby.

That's how my father always says it, like she went looking for a better place to camp rather than abandoning
a husband and son. She left us to go back to school in
another state and we haven't heard from her since she
left. "As if," I overheard my dad telling my grandpa
once, "raising a son and pursuing higher education
were mutually exclusive."

There's a lot of going back to school in my family.
Even my grandpa takes classes at the retirement community where he lives—bridge, computer program-
ming, and now he's starting to paint.

Dylan probably thought I was the greatest thing
ever. I don't think it takes too much to make his day,
though.

My father found him on the street, brought him
home and named him. But I feed him and de-poop the
yard. I brush the tangles and dead hair from his coat
and check him for fleas and ticks. I make him scrambled eggs and buttered toast when I'm sad because you
always feel better when you do something nice for
someone you love.

So that makes him mine.

He protects me. I haven't gone to the bathroom
alone since he came to live with us. I don't know what
kind of Evil Potty Monster he envisions, but he sits by
me when I pee to keep me safe from it. He sleeps on my
bed and growls soft and deep in his throat when anyone walks down the sidewalk in front of our house.

That makes me his.

The only bad thing about him is that he throws up if you feed him frozen waffles. But a little barf is a small price to pay for having such a great friend.

He's like a person to me except that he can't talk or read. But that morning, I wasn't so sure about that anymore.

I pulled the note from my pocket and read it again. *You're not as ugly as you think.*

That was the note I'd gotten from the dog a few minutes earlier.

As I had come out of the house to eat my toast on the front steps, Dylan had been standing there with the note in his mouth. He pushed at my hand with his nose to get me to take the piece of paper from him and wiggled his whole body in excitement, as if he *knew* what the words said.

Dylan's a border collie, so the whole note thing is not as out-of-the-realm-of-possibility as it first sounds. I'd read about a border collie in Germany who could understand a couple hundred words and knew how to figure out the name of something he'd never seen before by the process of elimination. "It's just a matter of time, my boy," Grandpa had said when I told him, "before that dog of yours has his own e-mail address, if that's the kind of bloodline he comes from."

My dad is not the note-writing kind. And who else could have left it for Dylan to find and give to me? Carl was off on his "custodial summer" with his divorced dad. Jamie was away at camp, and Christopher's school runs year-round. Matthew would just come out and tell me something, he wouldn't bother writing it down.

As I reread the piece of paper, Dylan nudged my hand with his nose. I looked at him, thinking.

"Did you"—I paused, looked around and then whispered—"did you mean it, Dyl?"

"*Woof*."

Sounded like a yes to me.

Dylan kissed my nose. Another yes. Then he leapt off the stairs after a rabbit that hightailed it around the corner of the house into the backyard.

It made sense that Dylan would try to cheer me up about how I looked. He'd been with me when I freaked out after I'd seen my yearbook picture on the last day of school.

Matthew, ever helpful, had said, "You're not completely repulsive, Finn. But I wouldn't worry about the girls beating a path to your door, either."

I looked up from the note. Nope. No girls headed my way. I read the note again and wished I could ask someone if I was really ugly, if I'd ever get any better-looking and, most important, if someday a girl would like me no matter what I looked like.

"Mind if we join you?"

I jumped at Johanna's voice and turned to see Dylan leading her toward me from the back of the house. She was wearing her wig. She sat next to me on the step, bumping my hip as she settled herself. Closer than I would have expected.

"Oh . . . hi . . . ," I said. "Dylan's supposed to stay on our side of the bushes. Did he go into your yard?"

"Not much of a yard." Johanna snorted. "I'm only house-sitting for the summer while the Albrechts are in Europe and I can't change anything about their property, of course, but oh, what I'd like to do with that space." She looked at the Albrechts' place and sighed.

"You garden?" I couldn't think of a more boring thing to do.

"Nope. Never so much as planted a single flower. But I can't stop thinking about having my very own garden these days."

"Then why did you move to a place where you can't have one?"

She didn't answer, instead looking around our yard. I followed her glance. While I kept the lawn mowed, we had no garden, unless you counted the straggly little bush thing called a hosta that grew around the mailbox, which, my father had said more than once, we couldn't kill with a stick.

"Do you have a job this summer?" she asked.

My mood took another dip. I didn't want to confess to Johanna that my only plans for the next three months involved reading as many books as I could right here on my front steps and avoiding people.

After an entire school year of eight classes a day, with thirty other students in each period, I figured I'd come into contact with two hundred and forty people each and every school day. And that's not even counting people on the bus, in the hallways and in the cafeteria. For a guy like me, that was sensory overload, and I needed to turtle up for a while.

I planned, in fact, to speak to fewer than a dozen people over the entire summer.

I'd figured that idea would work if I only went places with Matthew or my dad or grandpa and left the talking to them. I'd wear my iPod and a pair of sunglasses if I had to go anywhere alone, and act like I couldn't hear or see anyone.

Just meeting Johanna the day before, I'd already used up a third of my summer communications quota. And it was only the first week of summer vacation.

I doubted my dad and my grandpa would notice that I'd decided to limit my speaking, and Matthew had said he understood my plan.

What he actually said was "You've got the personality of a mushroom and that freaky idea of not talking to anyone creeps me out."

But I knew he had my back. I could count on him to run interference for me, at least for a little while. He's good like that. Even if he disagrees with you, he'll always help you out.

I realized Johanna was asking me a question.

"Would you like to work for me?"

No, not in a million years, I said to myself.

"Uh, what do you do?"

"I'm in graduate school."

Great, I thought, another one.

"Master of Library and Information Science. And I work at Anderson's Bookshop part-time. How would you like to plant a garden for me?"

No, not in a million, bazillion years. I cleared my throat and tried to think of a way to say no.

But somehow I didn't have the heart to come right out and tell her that digging in the wormy dirt and pulling weeds in the sun all summer long was not anything I'd ever want to do even if I knew the first thing about plants and flowers. Which I didn't.

"I thought you said you weren't supposed to do anything to your yard."

"Not my yard. Your yard."

"You want to hire me to plant a garden for you in my own yard?"

"I most certainly do. This house needs a garden, you need a job and I . . ." She trailed off. Something in her voice made me drop my eyes from her face. I looked at Dylan. When he saw me look at him, he put a paw on her knee.

She turned back and her eyes were bright. "So will you do it?"

"Yes," I said. "I most certainly will."

I would have said anything to make the sad look in her eyes go away.

3

We spent most of the rest of the day, the day that gave the world Johanna's Great Idea About the Garden That Was Going to Kill Finn, at the library.

There are literally hundreds of books about dirt.

Just dirt.

She took notes and made sketches and I tried to look interested as I paged through the first pile of books she'd shoved in my direction. But after barely getting through one chapter, I was so bored that I started alphabetizing the books she'd discarded so I'd look busy. I excused myself to go to the bathroom so many times I wondered if Johanna thought I had a bladder infection or an attachment to public restrooms. The librarian shelving books nearest the men's room started to look at me funny.

I finally headed over to the fiction section and took my time picking out the novels I wanted to read that week. I returned to our table with a bag of books; she hadn't even noticed I was gone.

I'd originally thought Johanna had a few rows of flowers in mind, but I soon realized that she aimed to smother every square inch of the yard under flowers, plants, shrubs, bushes, vegetables and something called container gardens. She sat muttering to herself, "USDA zones and plant hardiness . . . slope and drainage of the property . . . cliché of having upright plants on either side of the entry . . ." and so on.

A garden? This was a farm.

She showed me photos of bushes that had been trimmed in the shapes of animals and, for the first time all morning, I was kind of jazzed. I started reeling off cool ideas: pouncing tigers, bears standing on their back legs, huge spiders and killer sharks with wide-open mouths . . .

"That's not," she said finally, "the image we're going for."

"But the koi pond *is*?"

"I see your point," she said, making a big X in her notes. "You're signing up to be a gardener, not a fish wrangler."

I wasn't "signing up" for anything. She'd ambushed me, and I still couldn't figure out how she'd done it.

"Okay!" Johanna finally jumped up, stuffing her

notes in her backpack. "Enough for now. Let's get something to eat. How about Java Joe and Juice?"

"Um, I'm not really, you know, into organic fruit smoothies with bee pollen or whatever."

She laughed. "It was just a suggestion."

"I'm more a burger and fries or deep-dish pizza kind of guy."

"The Holy Trifecta of Grease, Carbs and Meat . . . I should have guessed. How about the burrito place around the corner?"

I nodded and we headed out and picked up Dylan. We'd tied his leash to the shaded bike rack behind the library.

Johanna ordered a grilled veggie burrito and I asked for a beef and pork burrito with extra cheese, sour cream, double guacamole and gut-busting-hot salsa. We ate at the outdoor table where we'd left Dylan. He scooted close to her chair, sensing a soft touch for scraps.

I'd inhaled most of my food before I realized that Dylan was getting most of Johanna's. Whoa. Beans. Beans + Dylan = Killer Farts. I'd have to open my bedroom window that night.

"Kinda sucky, huh?" I slurped my soda.

Johanna turned from giving Dylan another bite. "What's sucky?"

"Brown rice, whole-wheat tortilla, no cheese. I don't know how you ever thought you'd be able to eat something like that in the first place."

"A girl's got to watch her figure."

If she didn't have what my grandpa calls a good square meal pretty quick, her figure would disappear. I know from Jamie that girls think skinny is the way to be. But most guys like girls who aren't so bony and hyper about what they look like.

I worry about being fat, so I know how it feels, but I've never once skipped a meal, eaten a salad as a meal or weighed myself between doctor appointments, and I don't whine about my fat to anyone but Dylan and Matthew.

I dropped my plate next to Dylan so he could snuffle up the leftover bits. He cleaned the plate and hiccupped.

"Let's take a walk," Johanna said. "Dylan could use the exercise after his big meal and it's a shame to waste such a beautiful day."

I was just so glad she hadn't suggested going back to the library that I'd have done pretty much anything she said. We wandered down to the river that cuts through downtown and set out on the path along the water.

"So why did you move in next door?" I don't normally ask personal questions but Johanna was like Matthew somehow and I didn't feel too self-conscious talking to her.

"I'm twenty-four years old and I've been living in cinder-block dorm rooms and ratty apartments with weird roommates since I was eighteen. I didn't want to move back home with my folks because I've never had a place all to myself and I wanted my own space for a little while. Plus, it's close to school and free."

"Do you have family nearby?"

"You can't swing a dead cat in this town without hitting someone I'm related to by blood or marriage or friendships that go back forever. How about you?"

"Just my dad. Dylan, of course. And my grandpa lives nearby."

"That's all?"

"Grandpa says we're a family of men."

"Hmmm." She nodded. "My grandfather says we're a family of stark raving lunatics."

Just then I saw Karla Tracey.

She was sitting on a bench and glancing at her watch, waiting for someone. I couldn't help myself. I stopped walking. And talking. And breathing. I didn't, however, dive off the path and into the bushes to keep from being seen, which is what I would have done if I'd been by myself.

"Yoo-hoo. You in there?" Johanna had been trying to get my attention.

"Yes." I pulled my gaze away from Karla and looked at Johanna. "What did you say?"

"I asked if you knew that girl. From your reaction, that was a pointless question. What I should have asked was: How long have you liked that girl and why haven't you asked her out yet?"

"Like her . . . *Her?* . . . No, of course I don't like her, I mean, she's . . . well, *look at her.* She's perfect, and then . . . I mean, I'm . . . and she . . . I could never, not ever, not in a million bazillion quintillion years, ask her out, because—"

"Why not? She looks nice. Pretty hair, cute figure, she's not dragging around dead house pets and, since we're downwind of her, I can tell she doesn't reek of sewer gas and rotting flesh."

"No, she smells like cookies."

"Cookies! I've never met anyone who smelled like cookies. That must be wonderful."

"It is."

"Then why haven't you asked her out?"

I looked down at the ground. Embarrassed that Johanna didn't understand why a girl like Karla Marina Tracey would never go out with a guy like Finn Howard Duffy and wanting, more than anything, not to have to try to explain it to her.

I looked up at Johanna. She was frowning, eyebrows scrunched, as she studied my face.

"I could never ask Karla Tracey out. That would be . . ." I couldn't even *think* of how wrong that would be, much less put it into words.

"I think it's a waste *not* to ask her out," Johanna said. "And I hate waste."

"I'm . . . well, you know, I'm not good at talking to girls."

"We've been talking all day. You're doing just fine."

"Oh. I guess so, but normally, I mean sometimes, well, most of the time, when other people talk, I'm so worried that what I'm going to say is going to come out wrong that I can't focus on what they're saying and then I lose track of what we were talking about in the first place." I could see she didn't get it. I knew it: I really *am* the only person in the world who freaks out about something as simple as a conversation with another human being.

"Johanna, can we drop this subject? No offense."

"Sure. We have to get to the garden store to buy equipment anyway." We turned and walked back the way we'd come, avoiding Karla, but I saw Johanna glance back over her shoulder.

The sun was baking my skin. Bugs were feasting on the back of my neck. My lips cracked.

Sweat poured down my forehead, stinging my eyes. I could see blisters beginning to form on my palms. Dirt was caked under my fingernails. My shoulders were on fire from carrying equipment. My legs ached from kneeling on the ground. I was light-headed. Dizzy. Weak from exertion. I was starting to stink. I cursed my fate.

I'd been working in the yard for seventeen minutes.

It was eight-thirty in the morning and Dylan, no fool, was napping in the shade of the old sugar maple. I had never envied that dog more.

I looked around me and groaned: Our small yard had taken on epic proportions.

An hour earlier I'd been awakened by my dad

pounding on my bedroom door. I staggered out of bed, groggy because I'd stayed up most of the night reading. I was also surprised because Dad didn't usually wake me up in the mornings, not since I was little anyway.

"You have company." He grinned at me as I opened my door. Dylan streaked out of the room, skidded down the hallway and galloped downstairs to the kitchen. "It's the girl next door. She brought muffins. You'd better pull on some clothes and get downstairs before I eat them all."

Other than Matthew and my grandpa, I couldn't remember the last time we'd had someone over.

I grabbed a pair of shorts and a T-shirt off the floor, tugged them on and ran my fingers through my bed-head hair. I took a deep breath and hurried downstairs.

Johanna was sitting at our kitchen table talking with my dad like it was the most normal thing in the world. They were drinking coffee and Dylan had his head in her lap. The second I got to the table, she handed me a three-ring binder and a chocolate muffin, still warm and gooey from the oven.

"I made both of these for you," she announced. "One is the fruits of my labor at the library yesterday and the other is a bribe."

I took a big bite out of the muffin and set it down, licking the crumbs off my fingers as I paged through the color-coded sections of the binder. "Prep Work— Understanding & Improving Your Soil"; "Annuals &

Perennials"; "Trees, Shrubs & Vines (Hardy Greenery for Definition & Balance)"; "Lawns & Ground Cover—The Utilitarian Way to Achieve a Uniform Look"; "Watering, Feeding & Composting"; "Pruning & Propagating"; "Pests, Weeds & Diseases"; and "Year-round Tasks for Upkeep and Maintenance."

All in waterproof page protectors.

I took a smaller bite of the muffin, trying to make it last longer. Say a year. A perpetual muffin, I thought. That's what I need. My dad and Johanna were watching me chew.

"How"—I finally swallowed and spoke—"did you do this so fast?"

"I'm a supernerd about research and organization stuff. It's fun for me, relaxing, like a hobby."

I took a deep breath and flipped through the pages again.

She smiled and hopped out the door, waving good-bye to my dad and saying to me, "See you in the yard in a bit."

I looked at my dad. My dad looked at me.

He shrugged, gulped the last swallow of coffee and ruffled my hair. "I like her." He grabbed his car keys and headed out the door. "And I like the idea of a garden. I'd never have thought of it, so I'm curious to see how this project unfolds. Wake up Matthew before you start work, will you?"

So now I was crouching on the ground, the binder

in front of me, glaring at the stuff Johanna had bought yesterday after our walk by the river—hoses, trowels, rakes, a hoe, pruners, plastic trash bags, buckets, a shovel. Work gloves. And a red piece of machinery that looked like a lawn mower with teeth.

"You're such a wuss."

Matthew walked toward me, tool belt slung over his shoulder, beat-up work boots on his feet. We'd scuffed and scraped them with rocks the evening before because Matthew wanted to look like he fit in at the construction site. His dad had gotten him a part-time, unpaid summer internship, thanks to a pal in the business, and Matthew was getting on my nerves about it.

"My work will be backbreaking. Tough." He nodded. "Dangerous."

Right. I saw a long summer of running and fetching ahead of him.

"So," I asked, "you're off to grunt and sweat while holding sharp objects at tall heights?"

"Jealous, girly-man? I'll be running with the big dogs while you're planting petunias."

"Uh-huh. Five bucks says you'll be asking 'Do you take cream and sugar?' ten minutes after you get there."

"I might have to prove myself," Matthew allowed. "For a few days. You know, until the guys get to know me."

"Dream on. You're going to be the site scutpuppy and you know it."

Dylan had found a ratty old tennis ball, flung it at Matthew's feet and backed away. He dropped his head and shoulders, rump in the air, eyes fixed on the ball, waiting for Matthew to throw it for him.

Matthew heaved it straight at Johanna's house. Dylan went bounding after the ball, barking.

"Hey!" We heard Johanna laugh as she emerged from behind the bushes, Dylan at her side. Matthew's face lit up and he patted his tool belt as he stood. He'd told me once he'd read that when people flirt, they absentmindedly touch parts of themselves they want to call attention to. I looked down and kicked a clump of grass in disgust. I hadn't touched anything.

Johanna handed me her key chain. "I made you lunch and it's in the fridge—roast beef sandwiches, potato salad, watermelon and lemonade. There are fresh cookies in the jar on the counter."

Matthew frowned. I couldn't hide the smirk on my face. Score one for Finn.

"Won't you need your car keys today?" Matthew asked.

"No, I'm getting a lift."

"Work or school?" I'd told him about Johanna's classes and job.

"Playing hooky." She started walking away backward, still talking to us, as a small car pulled up in front of her house. "That's me; gotta motor. Finn, if you follow the daily checklists, you should be in good shape.

Matthew, good luck at your new job. Finn tells me you're in construction. Very sexy."

I glared at him. He flipped me the bird. We watched Johanna jump into the car and drive away.

"Real mature, Matthew, giving me the finger like that."

"Enjoy your cookies, Sally Mae."

"The cookies that Johanna made *for me?*"

He flipped me off again. Then we heard his dad's car honk out front; he was taking Matthew to work. Matthew waved and ran around the house.

The next eight hours were grim and sweaty. The gloves were too big to be any use and the Band-Aids kept slipping off. I wound strips of gauze around my palms and secured them with duct tape. "There's not a thing in this world, my boy," Grandpa always says, "that can't be fixed with duct tape."

Maybe I could duct-tape roses to the side of the house instead of planting the bushes.

The first day's first task was rocks. Or, as the binder read, "removing rocks to aid in prepping the soil." Easy-peasy, I thought, it's a yard, not a gravel road. I'll take a long lunch and get some reading done.

The tiller (that was what the red machine was) roared to life and I spent the rest of the morning shoving it in wobbly rows according to Johanna's sketches.

She'd wanted me to start with a patch that ran the width of the backyard because "southern exposure is the optimum for vegetables."

28

After the tiller had turned over the grass, I was supposed to crawl along with a bucket and remove the rocks.

At first I just tossed them into the bucket, but when it filled up, faster than I would have thought, I dumped them behind the garage in the alley. Our yard contained a trillion rocks.

Somehow the day lurched past, rock by miserable rock.

At the end of the afternoon, Matthew staggered into the yard and threw himself on the ground near where I was breaking up chunks of sod. I chucked my hoe off to the side and lay on my back near him. We both looked up at the sky and didn't say anything.

"If I work real hard," Matthew finally said, "and enough people quit or die or move to Uzbekistan, I might work my way up to the crappiest job in the world. Literally. Do you know, Finn, that someone is actually in charge of cleaning the Porta Potties?"

"Do you know that I am freaking out, Matthew, because I worked for eight solid hours and I'm still near the top of page one in Johanna's binder? And there are seventy-six pages. *Seventy-six!*"

We had nothing else to say.

My only thought was: Oh my god I hurt all over.

And judging by the grunts coming from Matthew, his was the same.

We finally got bored feeling sorry for ourselves and started comparing injuries and blood loss.

Matthew had been given one task that day—removing nails from old wood. Salvaged lumber was going to be used to make the new building look like an old building. Matthew said that added "prestige" to the structure.

Long story short, he'd picked up about seventeen slivers, banged his right thumb four times and cut his forearm on a nail.

The car that had come for Johanna that morning stopped in front of her house. She slowly pulled herself out of the passenger side, stood, braced herself against the open door and then pushed it shut. The driver beeped the horn and pulled away. Johanna started toward the house.

We got up and, following Dylan, jogged over to her as she made her way up the walk. "Dylan," I called, worried that he might knock her over if he jumped to kiss her face. But he pressed his shoulder against her knee and wagged his tail instead.

"You look awful," I said.

Matthew shot me a dirty look and said, "Finn means you seem a little tired."

"It hasn't been my best day."

"What happened?"

"I had chemo and broke up with my boyfriend."

Matthew and I looked at each other, then back at her.

"That was him," Matthew asked, "in the car?"

"*Was* being the key word, yeah."

"Are you . . . can we . . . I mean, you look . . ." I didn't know what to say.

"I didn't get much sleep last night, working on the garden binder and baking, plus I think I'm getting the flu. And, you know, I just got dumped. My mother is coming over after work but—" She doubled over and vomited next to the path, one hand clutching Dylan's neck. He stood still, looking up into her eyes, but I couldn't help taking a step backward and turning my face away.

"Man up," Matthew snapped at me.

When Johanna was done, he slipped an arm around her. She sagged against him and he jerked his chin at me. I jumped forward to hold her up on the other side. She seemed as light as air. Dylan led the way as we moved her into the house. As soon as we got her into her bedroom, she threw up all over herself and us and started to cry. I tried not to pull away.

Matthew grabbed a sheet from a stack of laundry in a basket near the door and threw it over her bed. We helped her lie down and he arranged a towel under her head. She was asleep before we'd even straightened up.

We stood watching her. Matthew took a deep breath.

"Go get clean clothes for us at your house."

I nodded and turned.

"We need broth," he said. "It's good for sick people."

"What's the difference between broth and soup?"

"Broth is soup juice, nothing chunky. If you don't have plain broth, cook a can of chicken noodle soup and strain the noodles out."

"Okay, what else?" I could hear the panic in my voice. I was amazed at Matthew's take-charge attitude. I wondered how he knew what to do and why I had no clue. Then I remembered that his grandma had stayed at his house after her hip replacement surgery. He'd helped take care of her.

Matthew thought.

"Tea . . . soda crackers"—he glanced back toward Johanna—"and towels and buckets or big plastic bowls. Oh, and call your dad if he's not home yet and bring him up to speed. Tell him we won't be home for supper."

"And what will you be doing while I'm running and cooking and searching and calling?"

"Cleaning up. Unless you want to trade?"

I slunk over to my kitchen. Dad was standing at the counter, chopping carrots for dinner.

"Hey, Dad. Do we have any broth?"

"What happened to you? Did you feed Dylan frozen waffles again?"

"No, it's, um, Johanna. The girl from this morning? With the muffins? She's, uh, sick, she had chemo and said maybe she's getting the flu." My dad frowned. "She got home a little while ago and now Matthew's over there waiting for me to bring broth and tea and crackers and clean clothes and—"

"Can I help?"

Help? Take over! I thought. I don't want to be anywhere near anyone who is hurling and crying.

"I think we've got it under control." I didn't believe that, but it was what Matthew would have said. Plus I didn't want to let Johanna down. "Her mother is coming over in a little while. If you could find the soup and stuff while I get cleaned up, that'd be great."

"Sure thing, son." He started rummaging through the cupboards but then turned back to me. "You're a good boy. I'll be right here if you need me and if her mother doesn't show up soon, come and get me. Be sure you and Matthew wash up well."

It was the longest conversation my dad and I had had in years.

I was back at Johanna's house fifteen minutes later, with a wagon full of clean clothes and every towel and large plastic bowl I could find. Dad had put hot broth in a thermos and we'd found another thermos, which we filled with hot tea. I had a big box of crackers, too, and pretzels and Popsicles and ginger ale.

"Sure I can't help?" he'd asked as I left.

"We got it covered. And it's only for a little while."

"I am definitely bringing supper over for you and Matthew when the stew is ready."

I wasn't sure I'd ever be hungry again, but I nodded.

I looked through the doorway of Johanna's bedroom and saw that Dylan had tucked himself into the curve behind her knees, which she'd drawn up to her chest. Matthew was sitting in a rocking chair next to the bed, holding her hand and singing, forgetting, as he always does, most of the words and filling in the missing parts with humming. I couldn't tell what he was singing; I never can. It's kind of nice, though.

He looked up.

"Hey. How's it going?" I pulled another chair up and handed him a change of clothes. He stripped off his shorts and shirt and shoved them into a bulging plastic trash bag next to him.

"I got her cleaned up." I was gratified that he finally sounded a little nervous. "I threw her clothes and the towels I used in that garbage bag. I think we should get rid of them. I don't want to see them again. I don't even want to know that they exist in the universe. Do you think we could burn them?"

"Hot water. Double detergent. Two times through the wash cycle."

We looked toward the voice and saw a curly-haired older woman standing at the door.

"What?" we both said.

"Give me the bag. I'll take care of it. You seem to have things well in hand here." She nodded to the wagon of provisions and to Dylan, whose tail went *thump thump* on the bed when she looked at him.

"I'm Matthew, this is Finn and that's Dylan." He handed her the bag. "You're Johanna's mom?"

She nodded. "Call me Pat. She mentioned she'd met the two of you. What happened here?"

We told her, and then she took the bag of laundry. We heard the washer start. She came back with a basket of clean stuff she must have pulled out of the dryer. Matthew reached over and grabbed a handful of towels and started folding. The three of us folded clothes while Pat asked us about school. Then she put her hand on Johanna's forehead.

"She's not warm and she's resting comfortably. And I smell something like supper in the air."

We followed Pat to the kitchen. I stopped dead when I saw my father and a pretty woman with long dark hair setting the table, talking and laughing. He pulled tinfoil off the tops of serving dishes and bowls.

"This is Fernanda," my father said when he noticed me standing there staring. "She's Johanna's sister from Brazil, and she's in the same master's program I am."

"But we never crossed paths until now," Fernanda added. "We ran into each other on the back steps; we both had the same idea to bring dinner over."

"How do you have a 'sister from Brazil'?" Matthew wondered.

"We've always had exchange students from foreign countries, ever since Johanna was a baby," Pat said. "Some of them, like Fernanda here, just never go back, and become our family."

"They have a very big family," Fernanda said. "Here"—she handed me a roll—"sit. Eat. There's enough here for all of us."

I couldn't take my eyes off my dad. He couldn't take his eyes off Fernanda, who was telling him about some problem she was having in a course. Matthew and Pat were chatting about his job; Pat worked for an architect and knew all about the building he was interning at. I ate my dinner but couldn't taste a thing.

I was thinking: Johanna was four, Pat was five and Fernanda was six.

After just three days, I was halfway through my summer limit of people I could talk to. If I kept hanging around Johanna, my plan to avoid people wasn't going to last long.

And I was surprised to find out I didn't much care.

6

I woke up the next morning on Johanna's living room floor with Matthew's right foot and Dylan's butt in my face.

After dinner, we had all cleaned the kitchen together. Johanna's dad, Dick, had shown up midway through dinner. He'd found the makings for S'mores in a cabinet. Soon we were trying to start a fire in the fireplace. We filled the room with smoke until we got the flue open and then we ate S'mores and watched the news. Well, Pat and Dick and Matthew and I did; my dad and Fernanda had gone over to our house to look through course catalogs. Or something.

Matthew fell asleep during the news. Pat pulled a blanket off the back of the couch to throw over him. "I'll get you a couple of pillows."

And just like that, we were spending the night at

Johanna's house with her parents, who wished me a good night and then went to the spare bedroom to sleep. I was exhausted from having been in the garden all day so I didn't put up much of a fight to go home. Plus, it was pouring rain outside.

When I woke up the next morning staring at and smelling weird parts of Matthew and Dylan, I rolled over and saw Johanna and her mother standing in the doorway watching us.

"Hey!" I bolted to my feet. "Johanna. How do you feel?"

"Better than you look. Where's the wolverine that made a nest of your hair while you slept?"

I nudged Matthew with my foot. He opened his eyes and said, "Did you rub S'mores on your head, Finn? You look weird."

"Get cleaned up and we'll have breakfast," Pat said.

When we got to the kitchen, Johanna was sitting alone at the table, finishing a piece of toast.

"Where are your folks?" Matthew asked, spilling cereal into a bowl.

"They saw that I was feeling better and left for work. My mom needs to grab some paperwork, then she'll be back."

I shoved two pieces of bread into the toaster, tripping over a pair of running shoes, and sat down next to Johanna.

"Pricy shoes," Matthew said. "Whose are they?"

"Mine. I'm training for a triathlon."

"You're what?" We had practically carried her up the front walk the day before.

"It's a fund-raiser for cancer research at the hospital where I get my treatments. I don't think I'm going to set any records. I just want to finish." She picked up the shoes and tried to untie a knot in the laces. She wiggled her chair closer to mine and set a shoe on my lap. "Can you untangle that for me?" She rested one hand on my shoulder as I worked.

"Hey," Matthew said, jealous. Johanna was flirting with me. Because if you touch a member of the opposite sex after you ask them for a favor, then you're flirting. It'd never happened to me, but I'd read about such things.

Matthew lifted the second shoe from Johanna's hand and set it on his lap. He pretended to be casual, but his cheeks got red. "So you're running to raise money?"

"Swimming, biking and running. Actually, it's a super-sprint triathlon. Shorter distances than a regular one. It's at the end of the summer at Centennial Beach and City Park. I have ten weeks to get in shape."

"Ten weeks?" Matthew sounded doubtful.

"I have proxies. A couple of my friends will do it for me if I'm not all buffed out and ripped by then."

Johanna was joking, but Matthew didn't smile.

"How much money do you have to raise?" I asked.

"There's no minimum requirement, but I'm hoping to get somewhere around ten grand."

"Whew." Matthew whistled between his teeth. "Are you going to ask everyone you've ever met for money?"

"Pretty much. Gimme your wallets." She held out her hand and grinned.

"How do you raise that much money?" I asked. She might as well have said a million dollars.

"I sent letters to everyone I know, and I've gone up to people at school and in the bookstore and asked for their support."

"I want to help," Matthew and I said together.

We all looked surprised.

"You do?"

"Sure," Matthew said. "We know people. Well, I do anyway."

"Shut up, Matthew," I said. "But I might do better with the letter-writing part."

"Are you sure?" Johanna asked.

"Yeah," Matthew said. "I can start by asking the guys at the construction site to chip in. We'll need to put together a presentation, though. With graphs and stats. They like stuff like that. And you should see the calendar in the manager's trailer. They like boobs."

Johanna threw back her head and laughed. "You've identified a target audience." Then she looked over at me with a raised eyebrow. "I have a three-ring binder you can share with them about the prevalence of breast cancer and how the money will be used."

"I can't work outside today anyway because the ground is muck from the rain last night." I looked out the window. "I can go with Matthew this morning and help."

We spent the next half hour going through Johanna's collection of facts and then Matthew and I wrote up notes on index cards. When Pat got back, Matthew and I headed out.

As soon as we got to the construction manager's trailer, some big guy in a yellow hard hat bellowed, "O'Malley! Haul your sissy butt to the donut shop for two–three dozen. No custard fillings this time, 'less you want us to get food poisoning when that goo in the middle goes off in the heat."

Matthew almost saluted. He hustled off the lot, leaving me in front of a group of huge men standing around the trailer. I clutched Johanna's binder and the stack of index cards in my sweaty hands. About thirty pairs of eyes looked at me.

One man finally grunted, "Kid. You here to help O'Malley pull his weight today?"

I dropped the index cards. I was going to have to wing it.

"Uh . . . no. I mean, not that I wouldn't like to work with you, because, of course, I would. Well, I don't mean of course, because I've never thought about construction as a career before because I'm only fourteen and I don't have a job yet, but . . . now that I'm here, it sounds like fun. I mean, not *fun*, because it's clearly dangerous what with all the . . . um, power tools and . . . everything, uh, else, but um . . . it sounds interesting and, well, let's see, inspiring. Is that the right word? You know, when you stop to think that you're *creating* something like . . ." I stopped. Several men were tipping their heads and squinting at me.

"What are you here for, then? What's with the notebook?"

"Well, see, we, Matth—O'Malley and I have this friend, well, our neighbor, no, *my* neighbor, because Matthew doesn't live with me, even though my dad says he's over enough to legally qualify as a member of the family, and if he were, then my dad could take the additional tax deduction—"

"Son," the guy interrupted. "You see this half-completed structure behind you? We've got a deadline, so spit it out and we can get to work."

I saw Johanna's face looking happy when Matthew and I'd said we wanted to help. I pulled myself together.

"Johanna, that's my neighbor, she has breast cancer."

They stopped sipping coffee and checking cell phones.

"That's a tough break, kid; she gonna be okay?"

"Oh, yeah. I mean, I sure hope so, because she's . . ." I remembered the binder I held and flipped it open, holding it up like a teacher reading aloud to a class. "The thing is—she's going to participate in a triathlon at the end of the summer to raise money to find a cure. The bar graph here shows how much she intends to raise, ten thousand dollars, and she's a little, well, a lot, actually, shy of her goal, so Matthew and I, well, just me right now because he went to get donuts"—I was starting to lose their attention—"we'reheretoaskyoutodonatemoneytohercause."

Dead silence.

I started to sweat. I'd just asked a bunch of men I didn't know for money and they were all standing there, looking at me.

I *knew* I should have stuck to my plan not to talk to anyone this summer.

I'm like a verbal machine gun when I get nervous. I mean, I know the power of words because I read a lot, but once I pull the trigger on them I can't seem to stop.

"Dude." A tattooed man three times my size lumbered forward. His nose ring caught the sun and there was a picture of a skull on his black T-shirt. He opened his wallet, which was attached to his jeans with a metal chain. "Here's something for your girl. My ma had that. She's all right now, but, man, that's one badass disease."

He handed me a hundred-dollar bill and thumped

44

me on the arm so hard it drove me sideways into a stack of lumber. He turned to his coworkers and boomed, "It's payday. Git yer cheap selves up here, you miserable tightwads, and give this kid a few bucks."

He stood next to me, watching as the men filed by, handing me wads of dollar bills, more fives and tens than I'd ever seen in my life, and a few fifties, too. Someone passed me an empty nail box to hold the cash.

It was all over in minutes and everyone went off to their jobs. I stood staring at a box of crumpled bills.

Matthew sauntered up with three boxes of donuts. "Okay, I'm back. We can go around now and I'll talk to everyone about the fund-raiser while you pass out donuts and then you won't even have to talk."

I held out the box. His mouth dropped open.

"What did you *say?*"

"Um . . ."

"Yeah, I thought so. But, man, just *look* at all that money. What great guys."

Matthew hurried to the office with the donuts as I picked up the index cards. Then we ran all the way back to Johanna's. She was curled up on the couch with Dylan and a book. When we burst into her living room, she looked up and pretended to be disappointed.

"You gave up already? I'd expected more from you boys, I really di—" I raised the box over her and dumped it. The money fluttered down.

45

"What did you do? Quick, lift your shirts so I'll know you didn't sell internal organs on the black market." She started collecting and smoothing out the wadded-up cash. "Is that a hundred-dollar bill? What *happened?*"

Matthew, who was picking money off the carpet, said, "Finn. It was all Finn."

Pretty nice of him to give me the credit. She turned to me.

"Matthew and I had worked out what to say. He had to go do his job, but I stuck to our plan and they just gave it to me. Really nice guys."

"That's for sure." Johanna made neat stacks of bills on her lap. "One thousand and forty dollars! You raised over a thousand dollars in one morning!"

"It's too bad we can't hang around bars," I said. "My grandpa says drunks are pretty free with their money. We could clean up at Frankie's Blue Room or Jimmy's Bar and Grille on Friday and Saturday nights."

"Finn! That's it. You're brilliant." Matthew had jumped to his feet, a big goofy grin on his face.

"Uh, I don't think bars are going to let us in, Matthew, and it wouldn't be smart to hang around in the dark outside with a box of cash."

"No. Not the bar idea. The grandpa idea. We should totally hit up the geezers at his old folks' home."

"You mean the assisted-living retirement community? Where my grandfather lives independently with his dignity and privacy intact until such time as medical or lifestyle assistance becomes necessary?"

"You memorized the brochure?"

"Grandpa threw the TV guide at my head when I called it an old folks' home."

"Whatever. Let's go ask them for money. It's . . . what did they call it in social studies? An isolated community. They'll be glad for the visit."

"We should really wait until Tuesday. That's apple brown Betty day in the cafeteria."

"What's today?"

"Rice pudding."

"Gag."

"Don't you have to get back to work?"

"Nah, they won't notice. To tell you the truth, getting the donuts is the biggest thing I do around there."

"Let's go right now; we can catch them after physical activity time. They're really mellow then."

"Who knew I'd moved next door to such natural-born hustlers?" Johanna mused as we rushed off.

7

Grandpa had an apartment in a cluster of buildings connected by walkways about twelve blocks from our house.

I visited him a couple of times a week (apple brown Betty Tuesdays and banana cream pie with chocolate curls on top Fridays) and he came over to our house for Sunday dinner.

We'd play cribbage or listen to baseball on the radio—he said television ruined the game; that if you couldn't be at the ballpark in person, you were better off listening to the color commentators on the radio and picturing the plays in your head rather than depending on "those talky morons on TV who don't know a force-out from a pop-up."

Mostly, though, we just hung out together reading. He always had a great mystery novel to share with me—he loved reading as much as I did.

Grandpa didn't have any brothers or sisters. And my dad was an only child, so I was his only grandchild. My grandmother had died before I was born.

"Finn, my boy!" Grandpa boomed when we knocked on his door. "It's rice pudding today. Matthew, always good to see you."

"Hi, Grandpa." I kissed his cheek and Matthew hugged him. "No dessert; we're on a mission."

"I thought you looked very purposeful when you walked in."

Matthew and I told Grandpa about Johanna and the race and the guys at the construction site. He nodded. "Follow me, lads, I know just who to speak to."

In the activity room he introduced us to a tiny woman in a purple tracksuit—Ruby, the social director. She took charge and led us to the gathering room, where a couple dozen people were playing bingo. She marched up to the caller and grabbed the mike out of his hand.

"Sorry to interrupt your game, but Josiah Duffy has a guest with something to ask. Finn." She held the mike out.

I remembered seeing a horror movie where the ground opened up and swallowed people whole. At the time I'd thought it was pretty scary. Right then, though, it seemed like a fine idea. I looked at Matthew, who shook his head and shoved me toward the microphone.

"Uh, good morning, I mean good afternoon, no,

wait . . . Not that it matters what time it is, well, it always does, matter, I mean, but . . ."

Words I didn't recognize came rushing out of me. I felt the sweat running down my sides, and the clenchy feeling in my stomach was making it hard to breathe. But then the image of Johanna sitting on her couch, money raining down on her as she smiled at me, filled my mind. I took a slow, deep breath.

"I'm Finn Duffy and I'm here to ask you to support our friend Johanna's pledge to raise ten thousand dollars for breast cancer research. Anything you can spare would help. Thank you for your attention."

"You there." An impossibly old lady crooked her finger at me.

"Yes, ma'am?"

"I don't normally appreciate being hit up for money, but that cancer—I had it once. They said I wouldn't make it." She was silent for a moment. "But that was twenty-some years ago and I'm still here. I'd like to meet this friend of yours. If I give you my winnings from today, will you bring her here?"

"Oh, sure."

She handed me a neat stack of money she hadn't stopped to count and squeezed my hand.

Matthew and Grandpa were working the other tables.

Ruby slipped a twenty into my hand. "Thank you for thinking of us. No one ever asks for our help. You did a good thing coming here today."

Grandpa drove us and an orthopedic shoe box full of money back to Johanna and Pat. After they had pulled him into a big hug, we counted out $224.

"You'd be wise to open a bank account," Grandpa told Johanna. "I don't know if Finn has mentioned it, but I worked at a bank, and I'd be honored to set things up for you."

"Wonderful! Thank you." Johanna handed him the box of neatly stacked bills.

The five of us toasted the official launch of Team Johanna with ginger ale.

Later that day Grandpa and Ruby distributed flyers that he'd printed up. The word spread and Johanna's bank account grew and grew.

"We are losing Matthew to the macho crap-heads at the site," Johanna told me a week after the start of our fund-raising campaign.

We were in the front yard, planting impatiens on either side of the front steps.

"What do you mean?" I asked.

"Last night at dinner all he talked about were ball-peen hammers and Phillips-head screwdrivers. I lost track of how many times he said 'It is what it is,' and I think we were"—she held up her thumb and forefinger millimeters apart—"this close to having him actually demonstrate how a 'bathroom bottle' functions."

"You should talk," Matthew said, suddenly appearing on the sidewalk as if out of thin air. "Did we not spend all Tuesday night discussing"—here he shut his eyes to think and recited—"snapdragons, Chinese forget-me-nots, California poppies and Madagascar periwinkle? Yeah. Good times."

He flopped on the ground and glared at the pots of impatiens.

"What happened at the site?"

"The boss brought his kid to work and I got stuck with him."

"You mean you were ba—"

"I was *not* babysitting!"

"No, of course not. What were you doing?" Johanna asked kindly.

"Technically I'm a floater—I go wherever they need me—but today I was floating in a sea of potty."

I smiled to myself. Now let's see who has the wussiest summer job.

Before I could rib him, he went on, "He knows squat about aiming. And his mother sent him to work with a backpack full of marshmallow and cereal treats and he bounced around on a sugar high."

He looked up at us from picking the calluses on his hands.

"Okay, so it was babysitting. But I didn't get eight bucks an hour, I didn't get a pizza delivered and I didn't get to watch cable I can't see at home."

"That's not all you do, right?" Johanna asked.

"I got to use the nail gun the other day and that was pretty awesome. I taped the safety lock and every time I pulled the trigger, the nails came out like bullets. I hit a signpost thirty feet away." He paused. "They don't let me near the nail gun anymore."

"But you know, Matthew," I said, "I bet no other freshman worked on a construction site all summer. You can say, 'I helped build that.'"

"Yeah. That'll kill Mike Gray—he still makes fun of the birdhouse I built in industrial arts."

"Hey! Can I have your birdhouse to hang in the tree over there? Mine turned out more like a bird shack that had been run over by a garbage truck."

"Sure." He was feeling magnanimous.

Johanna said, "We're on the same page: I just ordered a bird feeder and a birdbath."

Dylan barked.

"A doghouse," we all said.

"Why didn't we think of it before?" Johanna petted Dylan's ears.

Matthew said, "I can take a look at the remnant and discard piles at work and we can slap something together."

"You know what else I'd like?" Johanna asked. "Wind chimes to listen to as I fall asleep at night."

"I can make those out of old spoons," Matthew said.

We kept throwing ideas around. I was feeling great—everything was going well with the garden. I had the whole situation under control.

That was my first mistake.

My second mistake was deviating from Johanna's plan.

She was working at the bookstore the next afternoon when I needed to go to the garden store. I went by myself and bought supplies, borrowing money from our grocery fund. How hard could it be? I'd been doing this for about a week and was probably a master gardener by now. I bought the carrot seeds I needed and then, because the grass had been looking a little patchy, some fertilizer and a spreader. I also grabbed a few tiki torches that would look cool near the back gate. When I got home, I loaded the spreader with the proper amount of fertilizer. Then, for good measure, I dumped in a double dose. Twice as much, twice as fast.

I did the entire yard. I still had fertilizer left over, so I ran over the backyard three more times.

I went in to take a shower and start on the books that had been stacking up by my bed.

The next morning when I opened the back door, the stench hit me like a brick in the face. I ran through the house to the front steps, where I could breathe fresh air. Matthew heard me coughing and gagging from his room upstairs and came down to check on me.

"You okay?"

"Come here." We headed around the side of the house. Halfway around, he stopped. "Whoa. What *is* that?"

"I think there's something wrong with that fertilizer. It was on sale and I bet they were trying to unload it because it had gone bad. Does fertilizer even *have* an expiration date?"

"If it doesn't, it should."

"My eyes are watering."

"My lungs are burning."

"That can't be right."

Matthew pulled his T-shirt up over his mouth and nose as he wiped his eyes. "How much did you use?"

"The whole bag. I figured if a little was good, a lot would be better and maybe, you know, speed things up."

"I don't think it works like that."

"How do we undo it?"

"In science lab, Mr. Ferreri told me to dilute the problem when I added too much of something to an experiment. Maybe you can wash away some of the . . ."

"Reeking stench?"

"Yeah, can't hurt to try." He wished me luck and headed back upstairs—very quickly—to shower for work.

I got out every one of our hoses and attached them to the rotating sprinklers. Then I turned everything on full blast and went to sit on the steps with a book.

My third mistake.

"My boy, you've got to do something about Dylan," Grandpa called.

I looked up from my book. I could see from the angle of the sun that I'd lost track of time. Grandpa was standing on the sidewalk, looking at Dylan, who was covered in thick dripping mud. Dylan shook, sending globs of muck flying everywhere.

"Oh, no! The hoses are on!" I sprinted to the backyard.

A yard? No. A swamp.

I had completely flooded the backyard. The ground that I had tilled and hoed and raked and turned and fertilized was now a river of mud, oozing across the sidewalk and into the back alley.

The good news was that the stench of doom had lifted.

I finally read the fertilizer bag.

"Oh, no," I groaned.

"What?" Grandpa peered over my shoulder.

"One of the fertilizer's main ingredients is dehydrated steer waste, so when I added the water . . ."

Grandpa smiled.

". . . I made a yardful of reconstituted cow poop."

"Nothing like it for nutrients, my boy. You'll have a field of green in no time."

"I'm going to have to wait until the ground dries up and then go back to page one. I was all the way up to page twelve. All this time lost."

"Not all lost; the impatiens near the front door look good and the, um, organic waste product didn't seep toward either of the side yards. The rosebushes are safe."

"But the backyard is worse than when I started."

"You're going to have to resod the yard if you want to see grass this summer." Grandpa was studying the mud.

"I'm going to have to *plant grass?*" He nodded. "But I *had* grass, I *started* with grass, grass was the *one* thing that *was* growing in this yard before I began work."

"Think of it as starting with a clean canvas."

"Yeah. Okay. Onward. Oh, I meant to ask: How's your painting class going?"

"Pretty good. Mind if I bring my gear over and paint the yard?"

"You want to paint mud?"

"I'll be capturing the potential in its embryonic stage."

"You'll be painting mud, Grandpa."

"So I will, son, so I will."

"I could use the company." I looked around the yard and sighed. How was I going to tell Johanna about this? I grabbed a book and sat on the front steps to wait for her while Grandpa went into the house to start supper.

Johanna didn't get home until after dark so she took it surprisingly well. The moonlight didn't capture the complete and utter horror—a backyard that was four inches deep in cow poop. Plus she'd been out with friends and I could smell beer when she hugged me hello on the front sidewalk. "Don't stress about it, Finn."

I had opened my mouth to answer when I smelled cookies.

I looked past Johanna and saw Karla Tracey standing two feet away.

A car idled, waiting for her, at the curb. I stopped breathing. Felt dizzy. Johanna turned and smiled at her.

"Hi."

"You met my gran," Karla said to me, pointing to the car. A gray-haired woman smiled and waved. "At the center," Karla added, speaking now to Johanna. "She told me you were doing a triathlon to raise money for . . . I, um, wanted to make a donation and so we asked that lady at the activity center—Ruby, I think?—how to find you and she got your address from, um . . ." She stopped and held out an envelope to Johanna.

"Oh, honey, this is really kind of you. . . . What did you say your name was?" Johanna asked, knowing perfectly well what Karla's name was. Then she poked me. At least, I *saw* her jab me in the arm with her finger, but I couldn't *feel* it. I couldn't feel my head.

"Oh, sorry. I'm Karla Tracey. I, uh, hope it helps, it's not much, but . . . well, anyway, I have to get home now, Gran's waiting. She told me you're kind of, in a way, really, doing this for all women, I mean girls, or, you know—" She broke off and I could see her cheeks get red even in the light from the streetlamp. "Anyway, good luck."

She hurried to the car.

I felt the blood return to my feet, and the whole breathing thing, which is not as involuntary as they'd have you believe, started up for me again.

"Yeah," Johanna said, shaking her head, "I can see why you think you don't have anything in common with that girl." She started walking toward her front door. "If I close my eyes, it's like listening to you."

9

 My father opened a letter one evening after work at the beginning of July. He and I were sitting on the back steps with Johanna and Dylan. Matthew had gone to dinner at his mom's, and then to the movies with some girl he'd just met.

I was reading a note of my own. Dylan had shoved it into my hand when I came out to sit with Johanna and Dad. *You're wrong about you and girls.*

"How did *this* happen?" Dad sounded appalled.

"What is it?" I shoved my note into my pocket.

"As of this past spring term, I seem to have fulfilled all of my obligations. I'm done with school."

"And you didn't know?" Johanna asked.

"No. I've been going to summer term for a month now. I wasn't paying attention." He looked embarrassed. "I've been taking classes for so long now that I guess I lost track of time."

"That's pretty cool, Dad."

"It is, but I missed walking in commencement last month. I knew I should have read all those e-mails the registrar kept sending me."

"We should have a party!" Johanna said.

"We're not much for parties," Dad said.

"Well, I am. My Auntie Bean always says you should never pass up the chance to throw a party."

"Why do they call her Auntie Bean?" I asked.

"Anyone who can answer that question is dead. Auntie Bean is pretty old and we've always called her that and no one ever said why. You'll love her, she's a kick. And she makes the best cake."

"Cake?" Dad asked. He's got a wicked sweet tooth.

"Chocolate. You'll die, it's that good."

"I don't want to be any trouble."

"It's no trouble. My family throws parties at the drop of a hat. Or because it's Thursday and we haven't had a federally sanctioned day off for a while. It'll be nice to get everyone together for an actual reason."

"Do you . . ." Dad hesitated. "Do you think Fernanda will come?"

Johanna grinned. "She's the first one I'll call. Don't worry about a thing; I'll set everything up." She waved as she hurried back to her house, pulling her cell phone from her jeans pocket.

Two days later, we had our first party. Ever.

My dad invited his professors and classmates and some people from the clinic where he works. Grandpa

62

brought some of his buddies, and of course, Matthew and Dylan and I were there.

A ton of Johanna's friends and relatives showed up. It didn't seem to bother them that they'd never met my dad before. Everyone threw their arms around him in bear hugs, told him "Good job" and then set a covered dish or plate on the table. Fernanda, I noticed, hugged him a little longer than the others.

Everyone was very cool about keeping the party indoors, too, even though it got kind of warm in the house. Johanna must have explained that we couldn't take the celebration outside because of the state of the yard.

Auntie Bean brought the biggest cake I'd ever seen and Grandpa did a perfect double take when he saw her. Johanna caught the look and walked him over to make introductions.

Dylan trotted by with a hot dog in his mouth.

Music blared through the house—Bob Dylan, of course, since it was my dad's party. When "Visions of Johanna" played, I caught Johanna's eye and we smiled. Someone set up a chocolate fountain on the kitchen table; Matthew and Johanna's grandfather were cutting up bananas and skewering strawberries and chunks of angel food cake on wooden sticks to dip in the melted chocolate.

After a couple of hours, my dad handed me a wrinkled paper bag. "I asked everyone to contribute to your cause as they came in."

"You did this for me?"

"I'm proud of you, son. Real proud."

I looked over at Johanna, sitting cross-legged on the coffee table, surrounded by more people than we'd had in our house cumulatively in the entire time we'd lived there. She was balancing a spoon on her nose and reciting something. Maybe it was Shakespeare: "O for a muse of fire, that would ascend the brightest heaven of invention . . ."

It was nice. And it was a change. And it was all thanks to Johanna.

I went up to my bedroom and grabbed the book I was reading. I opened it and pulled out the bookmark I'd been using. I unfolded the piece of paper and read:

1—Dad. 2—Grandpa. 3—Matthew. 4—Johanna. 5 and 6—Johanna's folks. 7—Fernanda. 8— 9— 10— 11— 12— . . .

I saw in my mind the big guy with the yellow hard hat and the bigger guy with the nose ring from the construction site. And Ruby from Grandpa's assisted-living facility and the old lady who'd given me her bingo money. And all the people in my living room and kitchen.

I ripped the list up, let the pieces drop into my wastepaper basket and went back downstairs to the party.

10

 "What's this?" I asked. Johanna had thrust a fistful of papers into my face.

Grandpa and I were in the backyard late one afternoon. He was "trying out the new hammock," meaning he was sound asleep in the shade.

"These aren't more additions to the binder, are they? Because—"

"No," she interrupted me, "the university's arboretum is offering a gardening seminar this weekend. I want you to register."

"The what?"

She looked at the papers. "An arboretum is a living collection of primarily woody plants intended at least partly for scientific study."

"A plant laboratory?

"Sure."

"Never heard of it. Where is it?"

"Across town. If Matthew wants to go, I'll drop you guys off Saturday morning and pick you up Sunday after breakfast. You get to sleep *in* the arboretum."

"Uh, well, er . . . don't you think we're too old for . . . um, sleepovers?" I saw her fight back a smile. "The whole thing sounds kind of girly."

"Think of it as camping. More manly, right?"

"Uh . . ."

Johanna pulled another brochure from her backpack and handed it to me. "See," she said, "the program just screams Finn."

I read aloud. "'Spend a weekend sharing the wonders of nature. Designed especially for the serious gardener.' Are you trying to tell me I need help with the garden? I got the stench under control and the mud dried out. Things have been going really well lately. And the front and side yards look good. Anyone would say so."

"Not help so much as inspiration. You seemed a little dispirited by the stench and mud drama," Johanna said.

Grandpa came over and kissed Johanna on the cheek. She handed him a brochure.

I read the schedule:

SATURDAY

9 a.m.—Check in, pick up tent, meet hiking
    buddies, stow gear

66

9:30 a.m.—Welcome
10 a.m.–12 noon—Two 1-hour breakout
   sessions (see options)
12 noon–1 p.m.—Lunch
1–5 p.m.—4-hour intensive session (see
   options)
5–6 p.m.—Prepare dinner
6 p.m.—Dinner
7:30 p.m.—Twilight hike
10 p.m.—Campfire snacks, storytelling
   competition
11:30 p.m.—Lights out

Sunday
6 a.m.—Sunrise hike
8–9 a.m.—Breakfast and farewell

Hiking. Sleeping in a tent. Peeing . . . I wasn't going to think about that now but it was probably outside. Breakout sessions—just another way of saying classes. Homework, probably, or tests.

"How . . . um, did you find out about this?"

"Auntie Bean is working the conference."

"I'll go with you, my boy," Grandpa said. "Sounds fascinating."

Sounds like someone wants to spend more time with Auntie Bean, I thought.

"What's fascinating?" Matthew had come around the corner of the house.

"Spending the weekend with Finn and Mr. Duffy at the arboretum." Johanna handed him some papers.

Johanna and Grandpa started putting together a list of supplies and gear. Matthew was reading a brochure. He looked up, studied the yard and then stared at Johanna. He set the papers down and walked away to find Dylan's tennis ball to throw. I picked up the brochure, scanning the front flap:

The Arboretum's Tribute and Memorial Gift Program is an opportunity to honor the memory of a family member. Tribute gifts provide lasting recognition, and donors can select from trees, plants and flower beds.

I shrugged and put it back. What had captured Matthew's attention?

Matthew decided to come along, probably because of the pictures of girls in one of the brochures—high school cheerleaders did community service at the arboretum. Grandpa picked us up early Saturday morning and took us out to breakfast and we ate so many pancakes that I was ready to explode maple syrup. At the arboretum, we hustled over to the line at the registration table.

Grandpa spotted Auntie Bean handing out information packets and went to stand by her.

We chose our courses: It was a no-brainer that I had to go with the gardening offerings.

Matthew grunted, "Trees."

"How come?"

"'Cause."

I looked over and saw Kari Kelley, a girl from school, standing in the tree group, smiling at Matthew.

Grandpa, I knew, would head straight for "The Art of Nature: Sketching, Painting, Sculpting and Photography." He'd say it was because it would help him draw plants. But I couldn't help noticing that Auntie Bean was the group leader.

The rest of the day was a blur. I took notes until I thought my hand would cramp up and fall off.

During the first session, I learned to observe and identify a variety of trees, shrubs, perennials and wildflowers, which was cool because they gave us a handy little booklet with pictures.

The second session made my skin crawl—and I'm not kidding, because we discussed common pests. They tried to talk me into believing there was such a thing as a beneficial insect, but I wasn't buying it.

The afternoon was very helpful, even if I did sweat my guts out. They had us follow the groundskeepers around to help them pull weeds and deadhead the flowers and trim edges.

Standing there in the beds with plants and flowers all around me, I swear I got an inkling of the whole design thing and how texture and height and color worked together.

Johanna's binder had, of course, covered all this,

but I finally understood what she'd been going on about. Plus it was nice to see purple and orange and white and pink and red and green instead of my garden, which was nothing more than dirt and wilted grass.

I ran off to catch up with Matthew and Grandpa for dinner. Well, Matthew anyway; Grandpa said his bones were too old to sleep in a tent and that Auntie Bean was driving him home. After they stopped for dinner, of course.

Matthew and I looked at each other. Of course.

We tried to help with the grilling, but after we each dropped about a pound of hot dogs in the coals, we wound up pouring lemonade.

We scarfed our food. Matthew couldn't wait to hit the hiking trails. He wanted to take a quick hike and then be back in time for the campfire and a seat next to Kari.

At first it was really nice. Quiet. Pretty. Peaceful. Matthew had the map so I just followed him and didn't pay much attention to where we were headed. He said we'd get a better sense of the place if we avoided the marked paths and trails. And, like the moron I sometimes am, I didn't question him.

Until we'd walked about seven hundred miles.

"It's getting dark, Matthew."

"That's why it's called a twilight hike."

"Do you know where we are?"

"Not exactly."

"What does that mean?"

"That I know we are somewhere on the seventeen hundred acres of arboretum property. I also know that it is completely fenced in, so, worst-case scenario, we walk until a fence stops us and then follow it to a gate."

"Then can we go home?"

He stopped, studied the map, looked around, peered at the map again. "Ah, I see; we're not far from the marsh/slough/swamp/wetland area."

The next step I took filled my hiking boots with slushy ooze.

"I think we're already there."

"Oh, good, then we take a left."

"A left?"

"According to the map—no, wait, it was upside down. Okay, left is out, right is in. We go right. We definitely go right and we'll hit the path that leads us to the maze. And then the children's garden, the conifer walk and the lake. We head toward Visitor Station Four and follow Meadow Trail back to our campsite."

"There's not a shortcut?"

"That *is* the shortcut."

"Sounds like we may die before it's over."

"Nah. We're practically at the tent already."

"Hey—a bear!"

"It's a tree."

"We've been walking for two hours."

"Two and three-quarters."

"Do you suppose a rescue team might come get us if they notice we're not back at camp?"

"Your dad signed a waiver of responsibility so no one's going to worry about us."

"Are those vampire bats in the branches up there?"

"Sparrows."

"Eww . . . did I just step in—"

"Scat. Yes. Leave it to you that the only sign of wildlife you actually do find is poop."

"What kind, do you think?"

"Does it matter?"

"I guess not," I sighed.

We hiked. Then we just walked. Finally we plodded. When I was about to throw myself on the ground and crawl, we stumbled onto the tent site.

Pitch-black and dead silent. We'd been gone so long, we'd missed the campfire and the storytelling and the S'mores. And Matthew's chance with Kari. I was too tired to be bummed. We pried our boots off our swollen feet and fell asleep.

"Rise and shine, monkey butt!"

I swear I'd only just lain down and closed my eyes when Matthew bellowed at me. I pried my eyes open.

"What time is it?"

"Five-forty-five."

"In the morning?"

"No, in Namibia. C'mon. Sunrise hike!"

"You're kidding. We just got back from the twilight hike and you want to go out there again?"

"*Get up!* Kari's already talking to the leader."

I sucked wind pulling my boots back on over my feet, which looked like bread dough, and I almost peed when I shoved my right heel down. Even Matthew had tears in his eyes when he tightened the laces on his boots.

My feet hurt so bad that my memory of the sunrise hike is a swirly loud orange pounding buzz in my head. I trailed really far behind. I also sat a lot and made sure I never lost sight of the tents.

Matthew perked up as soon as he joined Kari for the hike. The last I saw of them, they were headed into the woods and he was making her laugh.

At breakfast, I lay on the ground and put my feet up on the bench of the picnic table. I'd heard once that elevation was good for injuries that involved swelling. And probably for feet that kind of squished and gushed with each step. Matthew dropped a piece of toast on my chest as he walked by to take Kari more orange juice.

When Grandpa picked us up, I crawled to the car.

11

 Monday morning, I went out to the backyard and bellowed. Matthew came running downstairs and out into the yard.

"What happened?"

"While we were away this weekend, the rabbits ate my garden. And Dylan must have just sat there and watched, like it was doggy TV or something. Doesn't he have some kind of instinct about things like this?"

"I bet if a flock of *sheep* had wandered into the yard, he'd have done something."

"Oh, well, fine, then. I don't have to lie awake worrying about an infestation of sheep. Good to know."

"Um, Finn?" Matthew asked. "How can you *tell* that the rabbits ate your garden? I don't remember there being much there for them to eat."

"Shoots. I had shoots, Matthew. Only about four of them, I know, but still. And look at all the bunny footprints. It's like they had a gang rumble or something in my garden." I stomped out of the yard.

We had a quick breakfast with my dad and then he gave Matthew a ride to his job.

I didn't do anything in the yard that day; instead, I copied my notes from the weekend into the binder. When I was done, the binder had bloated to 126 pages.

I had a moment of panic just holding the weight of it in my hands, but then I realized that the binder had become a book: Johanna and I had written a book about our garden.

Books make me feel safe. Books make me feel normal. And now, I guess, so did working in the garden.

I stood up, stretched and went to the kitchen to make pasta and brownies. We'd take them to Johanna's house for dinner so Matthew and I could tell her about the weekend. I could show her our book.

Matthew appeared after work with a small tree in each hand, their roots wrapped in burlap. "They're for the garden. Sven from the site took me to the nursery after work and then gave me and the trees a ride home."

"You bought them?"

"Yeah."

"How come?"

"'Cause."

"Oh. That's really nice. Where should we plant them?"

We decided on a spot in the front near the sidewalk.

When Johanna got home from a run with some friends, we showed her the trees. Then we ate and paged through our book together. She laughed until milk came out of her nose when Matthew tried to describe the twilight hike.

When we were cleaning up from dinner, she said, "Another round of chemo coming up this week."

Matthew dropped the plate he was drying.

I stared stupidly at the pieces on the floor. Johanna stood frozen next to the sink. Matthew was breathing hard like he does after a track meet. Dylan tried to pick up a piece of the plate with his teeth and then swiped at the mess with his paw.

Johanna squatted and studied the pieces.

"Look—Dylan made a pink ribbon."

She stood up, reached into the cupboard and pulled out the pile of pink plates. One by one, she dropped them on the floor in front of her. Dylan yelped and ran to the living room. Matthew and I watched her break seven plates, one after the other.

Johanna stood looking at the pile of shattered plates. Then she took a deep breath and spoke.

"Don't worry. Those were *my* junky plates. Let's go. Alice Johnson's Antique Corner is open until eight or nine on weeknights." She grabbed her purse and car keys and looked at us. "We're moving out now."

"Uh . . . Johanna?" I said. "Where are we going?"

"On a quest."

"For what?"

"Art. Beauty. Truth. Pink plates."

"You want to buy more pink plates?"

"Yes."

"Are you going to break those, too?"

"No. *We're* going to break them. Are you in?"

"Yeah." Matthew practically leapt across the room to follow her out to her car.

"Matthew?" I called. "What's she talking about?"

"Art. Beauty. Truth. Pink plates."

I rolled my eyes and followed.

We found half a dozen plates and bowls. They didn't match, but they were pink. We picked up the pieces from Johanna's floor and put them in a box. She didn't seem to want to explain, and Matthew was acting all smug like he was in on what was going on or it didn't bother him that he didn't know, so I just kept my mouth shut.

The next morning when I was in the garden, Dylan dropped down in front of me and woofed, but the sound was muffled by the piece of paper he had clenched between his teeth. I pried it out of his mouth and read: *The truth always reveals itself, and usually in mysterious ways.*

"You're getting pretty philosophical, Dylan."

He yawned.

I petted his ears while I looked at the note. When the dog spit had dried enough, I folded it, slipped it into my pocket and went back to work.

Over the next week, Johanna bought more pink

plates. When she needed to rest after chemo, she had Grandpa and Auntie Bean take me and Matthew to a couple of flea markets. The boxes of plates on Johanna's basement steps filled up.

One night when I was trying to fall asleep, I remembered a box in my own basement. I went downstairs and ripped open the top and saw a gift card: *To Kathy and Rich: Happy wedding, happy life. Love, Mom and Dad.*

Rich is my dad's name.

I pulled the packing material aside and saw pink flowers on a platter. I nodded to myself.

Then I dragged the box up the steps and out to the garage. I unwrapped twelve big plates, twelve little plates, twelve cups and saucers, twelve bowls and a bunch of serving pieces.

I stood there looking at them lined up on the garage floor and then, one by one, I picked up each plate and dropped it.

My grandfather had said once that he worried I might have unresolved hostility about my mother's abandonment. I guess he was right.

I swept up all the pieces, dumped them into the box, dragged it over to Johanna's back porch and went to bed.

She didn't say anything about the box the next day, just handed Matthew and me two pairs of safety goggles and two hammers and led us to a work table in the basement where she had set out all the unbroken china.

"Smash 'em, boys," she said.

And so we did.

When we were done, we found her in another part of the basement, mixing up a big bucket of gray glop.

I saw twenty-four wooden frames, about eighteen inches square and two or three inches deep.

"What's all this?" I asked.

"Stepping stones for the garden. That's what the concrete and frames are for. I ordered the frames from a catalog. We're going to make mosaic designs in them with the broken dishes. The pattern is pink ribbons." We looked blank. "Because that's the symbol for breast cancer awareness."

"Oh." I looked away and felt a little sick. Aware. Right. I wished there was a symbol for ignoring. Breast cancer avoidance. I wondered what color that ribbon would be.

Matthew took the stir stick from her hand and began mixing. Then we went from one frame to the next, lifting the bucket together and carefully filling each frame with the concrete. We taught Dylan how to walk behind us and quickly press his paw into each corner. Then Matthew held him still while I picked gooey concrete from between his toes before it dried.

The night Johanna decided the concrete had "cured," we crawled along the floor using stinking adhesive to secure the broken china on the hardened concrete in a pattern of pink ribbons.

A day later, we grouted the pieces of china. A week after that, we pulled the stones out of the frames and scrubbed the excess grout off.

One by one, Matthew and I carried the stones to the backyard, and then we argued about where to set them in the grass.

I studied the yard. "If we make a curve from the front sidewalk to the back walkway, it might look like a *J*."

"Let's spell out *HELP*," Matthew said. "Then maybe a garden fairy will read the message and fix everything. I don't mean to be bustin' you, buddy, but that's probably your best bet for this place shaping up."

In the end, though, it was Matthew who measured the space and laid the stones and made the giant *J* for *Johanna*.

12

 Mornings had become my favorite part of the day. I'd get up before Dad and stand on the back steps looking at my garden coming to life as the sun rose.

Today I scratched my arm as I looked over the yard.

I scratched my thigh and squinted at the vegetable patch.

I scratched my shoulder and glanced at Johanna's house.

I suddenly realized that I was scratching my *whole entire body*. And that I couldn't stop.

I ran upstairs to the mirror. I was covered in angry red blotches. I looked down, gingerly, *everywhere*. I grabbed the bag of cotton balls and the bottle of calamine lotion and got to work.

Dad and Fernanda were sitting together at the

kitchen table sharing the newspaper when I came back downstairs. She'd brought fresh rolls for breakfast.

"You look concerned, son."

"I think I've been watering poison ivy."

"You're joking."

"Uh, no, and if you'd look at the calamine lotion on every square inch of my body, you'd realize that."

"How did this happen?"

"A couple of days ago I was cutting through the empty lot on the way to Grandpa's and I saw this clump of leafy stuff that looked really healthy, and *nothing* in our yard looks that good. I felt bad about how much this whole thing is costing Johanna and this was free, so I dug it up and planted it over near the corner of the house and now I think I'm dying of itch."

Dad led me back upstairs to the bathroom. "Let's check for rash and blisters in places you can't see."

Fernanda got online to look for cures and then came upstairs and stood outside the door as Dad dotted calamine lotion on my butt.

"You'll be crusty and oozy for two or three weeks, and you might try applying the gel from an aloe vera plant to the affected areas," she called through the door.

Dad and I looked at each other and shook our heads. No more plants.

Dad and Fernanda left for work and I went to sit on the front steps. Trying not to scratch.

"You look glum. And, um, polka-dotty." Johanna stood at the bottom of the steps.

"You know our book?"

She nodded.

"Well, we might have to title it *The Hopeless Gardener: How to Turn a Perfectly Fine Backyard into Smelly Mud, Food for Wildlife, and Toxic Greenery.*"

"Fernanda called me from the car. I'm sorry about the poison ivy."

"Johanna?"

"Yes?"

"I have a black thumb."

"What do you mean?"

"Have you noticed that the backyard, um, still kind of stinks a little if the wind is right and that nothing is really growing, except, of course, for the worm and mosquito and wasp and rabbit populations and, of course, the itchy blisters on me? And I swear the rocks are reproducing behind the garage in the alley."

"And?"

"Well, I mean, it's not exactly what you had in mind, is it?"

"Not at all."

"You look . . . happy about it."

"It's turning out so much more interesting than the original plan, Finn."

"Oh," I said. "That's a relief." Then I remembered. "Speaking of the plan, I meant to tell you that we collected about three hundred dollars yesterday."

"How'd that happen?"

"I was in the front yard and two girls from school, Sophia and Lydia, showed up. Sophia's mom works at Dad's clinic and Dad got the staff and patients to start dropping loose change in an old water cooler bottle. When it was filled, they took it to the bank and had it converted to bills."

Johanna laughed. "You may not be a natural gardener, but you've got a real knack in terms of inspiring others to raise the *money* kind of green."

I stopped to think. Really? Maybe so. Matthew and Johanna and I had been finding envelopes of cash and checks, a couple of bucks here, five or ten dollars there, slipped under our front doors, in our mailboxes and under the windshield wipers of Johanna's car.

Somehow I itched a little less and the yard didn't look so hopeless.

13

 Late one afternoon a week later, Johanna called from her backyard as she headed into mine. "You have a date tonight!"

"What are we doing?"

"Not we. You. You have a date tonight."

She saw my face as she got to me, and draped an arm around my shoulders, pulling me in for a half-hug. "Don't look so scared. Dates are fun."

"Fun. They're fun. You think they're fun."

"Most people do."

"What are you talking about?"

"I arranged a date for you because I didn't think you were going to do it on your own. That pretty girl from the river walk who stopped by with money awhile back came into the bookstore today and I helped her pick out a few books—"

Girl from the river walk.

My mind was moving too slowly.

"—and so we got to talking and I asked if she had a boyfriend and she said no, so . . ."

It finally dawned on me.

"You set me up on a date with Karla Tracey." The pounding in my head made it hard to hear my own voice.

"Yes, I did." Johanna looked maddeningly pleased with herself and I wanted to put her in what my dad used to call, when I was little, the naughty chair. She needed to reflect on what she'd done and then apologize.

"I thought . . . I thought you knew that, I mean, can't you understand how . . . well, she and I are just not . . . Johanna, I can't go out with a girl like that."

"You can and you will."

I was completely terrified.

And yet there was a tiny thrill, too.

"What did she say when you asked her out? Uh, for me, that is? Does she even know who I am? What if"— I started to panic—"she said yes thinking you meant someone else and then, when I show up, she takes one look at me and realizes her mistake and I'm just standing there not knowing what to say because you know I can never think of the right thing to say in a normal situation much less something as horrible and weird as this and it'll just be awkward and embarrassing for both of us and the moment will drag on forever and then . . ." I ran out of steam.

"Then what? This is a fascinating, if highly unlikely, scenario. You know that, don't you?"

"No. That's exactly how I see things playing out."

"Would you," she said in a serious voice, "do it for me, Finn?"

"Go on a date with Karla Tracey for you?"

"Yes."

"Why?"

"I wanted you to make a garden for me, too, and that's working out pretty well, isn't it?"

"Well, when you put it that way . . ."

"I called Matthew after I spoke to Karla. He's on his way over."

"For what?"

"To keep you from running and hiding."

I looked at her. She looked at me. Then she smiled. "It'll be great."

She turned and walked back to her house, running into Matthew at the corner of our yard. They nodded at each other. Matthew headed toward me, a paper bag in his hand.

"Rocking news, Finn—Karla Tracey." He whistled between his teeth.

"Can you even believe it?"

"Nope. Not really, but stranger things have happened, I guess. I mean, that's what my mother always says anyway. C'mon, get your stinky pits in the shower."

I stood in the shower until the water ran ice cold. Maybe I'd wake up and realize this was not really happening to me.

When I finally stepped out of the shower, shivering and a little blue, Matthew was sitting on the bathroom counter reading the back of a small tube.

"What's that?"

"Self-tanner."

"What's it for?"

"You."

"Me?"

"Let's face it, Finno, tan fat looks better than pale fat."

"I'm *not* fat."

"You're not tall and thin, either. No matter how tall you stand or how hard you suck in your gut."

It was at times like this when I wished Matthew didn't notice so much.

"And besides," he said as he tossed the tube to me, "you still have a few poison ivy scabs that could use camouflaging."

I read the directions out loud. "'For best results, exfoliate well before applying product.' What's 'exfoliate'?"

"To remove rough, dead skin."

"Why would I have rough, dead skin and how do you know these things?"

He shrugged.

"I think I'm pretty . . . smooth and . . . undead. Can't we just skip that part?"

"Yeah, just smear it all over like sunscreen; we don't have that much time anyway."

After I applied the "product" wearing the plastic gloves included with it so I wouldn't "stain or discolor" my palms, which made me wonder what was going to happen to the rest of my skin, Matthew and I waited for me to dry, like a wall we'd just painted.

We decided I'd keep things low-key. He and Johanna thought I should suggest to Karla that we go to the free outdoor concert the city band put on every Thursday in the summer. Matthew and Johanna would be there, too, so I'd have backup nearby. "You know, in case you melt down and need to be rescued."

"Thanks for the vote of confidence."

He looked at his watch and jumped up.

"Dude. We gotta get you dressed." He poked me in the arm. "Ugh. You're still tacky. Here, let's use the hair dryer to speed up the drying."

This is not going right, I thought, but I stood with my arms outstretched and my legs spread wide and Matthew pointed the blow-dryer at me.

"This is not good," he said finally when he'd clicked the dryer off and studied me.

"What's not good?"

"Well, the heat from the blow-dryer seems to have caused an adverse reaction with the chemicals and—

now, don't freak out, Finn, but you're not exactly 'golden brown' like the tube says. It's more like, um . . ."

I wheeled around to look in the mirror. "Orange. I am the color of orange sherbet."

"Maybe just a little."

I dove into the shower and blasted the faucets on, forgetting that I'd used all the hot water. I howled when the icy cold needles hit me, and scrubbed my entire body frantically with a washcloth. I had to be scraping the tanner off because I felt like I was removing all the layers of my skin.

I stepped out of the shower and looked in the mirror.

Orange.

Only now I was shiny clean, too, with a pink tinge from all the scrubbing.

"Long sleeves," Matthew said, nodding. "And pants. That'll work."

"It's eighty-nine degrees outside."

"And you have orange and pink skin with crusty scabs."

"Good point."

I got dressed and we agreed that, for me, I looked okay. Except for my face, but I vetoed Matthew's plan to get Johanna over with her makeup bag to try to "powder down" the color.

Finally, I took a deep breath. "Let's do this."

14

 Johanna was sitting on the front steps waiting for us. She did a double take when she saw me, but she didn't say anything even though I looked like a highway caution cone. Then the three of us walked over to Karla's house.

Silently.

I don't know about them, but between the long sleeves and pants and my nerves, I was sweating buckets, and I kept glancing at the bushes on the edge of the sidewalk in case I needed a convenient place to barf.

While Johanna and Karla were talking at the bookstore that afternoon, they'd arranged that I would pick Karla up at seven, and Johanna had gotten the address and directions. I could have saved her the trouble; I knew that Karla's house was exactly three hundred and ninety-four yards from my house and that the numbers in her address added up to seven, my lucky number.

We came around the corner of Karla's block and Matthew and Johanna gave me one last critical look. Johanna smoothed my hair off my forehead. "Now, Finn, tonight is about having fun. Talk to her like you do me and you'll be fine. And remember that people will always think you're fascinating if you show that you're a good listener, because everyone's favorite subject is themselves. Ask her about her interests and hobbies and pets and family and friends and favorite classes—actually, ask her about her favorite *anything* and you're good to go."

"That's it?"

"What's it?"

"That's how you talk to people? Ask them about themselves?"

"It's one way."

"I wish," I said, glaring at Matthew, "someone had told me it was that simple a long time ago. He could have saved me a lot of worry."

"Hey, don't look at me," he replied. "I'm always too busy dazzling people with tales of my wonder and might to notice if they have much to say or not." He punched my shoulder, but I could tell he was impressed with Johanna's advice too. "See you at the concert. I'm meeting Kari there. Have a good time."

They disappeared around the corner, heading

toward City Park and the bandshell three blocks over. I looked at Karla's house.

Silence.

House just sitting there.

Matthew and Johanna were out of sight and I thought about what Johanna'd said. I stood tall, or as tall as I could, and sucked in my gut. Then I marched up to Karla's house.

She must have been standing behind the door because it flew open before I pulled my hand away from the doorbell.

"Finn?"

"Karla?" Genius. Who else is going to answer the door at her house? I started to perspire again and a faint wave of nausea hit my gut.

Then she smiled at me and I felt . . . wonderful.

Karla was smiling at me.

Me.

Finn Howard Duffy.

And she knew it was me, too. She hadn't screamed or pretended not to speak English or to have amnesia when she saw me. She looked . . . she looked kind of glad to see me.

"I love your friend Johanna." She was talking very fast, the way I do when I'm nervous. "It was great to talk to her today."

"Johanna . . . Johanna is . . . the best person I know. And she's always got the best ideas. She . . . um . . . she said I should ask you if you wanted to go to the concert in the park."

Karla nodded and called goodbye to her parents in the back of the house. We walked over to the bandshell. We'd gone a block and a half without speaking and I was starting to feel that clutchy panic again, the kind that made it hard to breathe and see and stay upright, but I forced myself to turn to Karla and say, as if I talked to the most beautiful girl I'd ever seen in person or on the movie screen every day of my life, "So, tell me what you've been doing this summer."

And she was off, talking a mile a minute about hanging out at the mall with her girlfriends and learning how to knit with her gran who was visiting from Phoenix and her aunt's brand-new baby who, she said, looked weird and smushy only she wasn't allowed to say that out loud or her parents swore she wouldn't get her allowance until she was thirty. She talked all the way to the park and while we were finding our seats in the grass and right through the concert.

And Johanna had been right: If I listened to Karla and asked questions about what she said, I didn't have any problem talking. There weren't any of those horrible silences where you can hear the blood rushing through your veins.

During the third or fourth song, the people next to us shushed us. Karla looked embarrassed. She looked, in fact, like I always feel. I gestured with my head: Let's go.

We ducked out of the concert and walked downtown. Good thing Matthew had reminded me to bring my wallet. When I saw the ice cream place, the kind where they mix the toppings in the ice cream on a slab of frozen marble, I asked, "Do you want a cone?"

We decided to share a mondo sundae and drove the poor guy who worked there crazy adding more ingredients until we wound up with a bowl full of graham cracker crumbs, mini-marshmallows, baby chocolate chips, chocolate syrup, whipped cream, almonds and bananas over triple-chocolate-chunk ice cream.

Karla dug right in. "You're really easy to talk to, Finn," she said, licking her spoon. "Most people are so busy thinking about what they're going to say that they never really listen to what you're saying. Do you get what I mean?"

"Absolutely." If she only knew.

"But, well, you're a really great listener. I mean, Johanna said you were and—"

"She did?"

"Yeah, she said you were a really great guy who just needed a chance to prove it."

"That sounds like her."

"And then she told me you're the kind of boy I should be getting to know; that good guys like you who can be good friends are way better than—" She stopped and looked uncomfortable.

"Way better than popular guys who are good-looking and self-confident?"

"Uh . . ." She poked at the ice cream with her spoon, avoiding my eyes. Then she looked up at me, took a deep breath and said, "That's exactly what she said. And that I could do better for myself than to fall for the outside of someone when it was their insides that really counted."

"Did she say it would be a waste if you didn't?"

"How did you know?"

"Waste is a big thing for Johanna."

Karla stared down at the table for a minute. "How does she come up with all these things?"

"I have absolutely no idea; I'm just glad she tells me what she's figured out."

Out of the corner of my eye, I saw Matthew sitting three tables over with Kari. He waved. I figured he and Johanna had agreed that he'd keep an eye on me.

I don't know if it was that my first date was going so well, all the ice cream that was melting in my gut or the way Johanna had known I'd have a good time on a date with Karla, but I had never felt more right in my skin in my whole entire life than I did at that moment.

15

 I didn't sleep very well after my date so the next day I was out of bed and downstairs early to get started working in the garden.

I took one look and ran back upstairs. I pounded on the guest room door like a maniac. Dylan added to the chaos by barking and jumping up and down. It briefly crossed my mind that we might wake up Dad, if not the rest of the neighborhood. Matthew threw open the door and squinted at me, half asleep.

"This better be good."

"Come see," I said. I dragged him to the yard and pointed at the tiny green buds poking out of the black dirt.

Matthew shrugged. "You got me out of bed for this?" He poked at the seedlings. "What's the big deal? Weeds do it all the time."

"Well, yeah. Yeah, but I planted these from seeds and now they're buds."

"Wow."

The nasty tone of his voice, so un-Matthew-like, made me take a step back.

Then he rolled his eyes.

I went from pride to anger in a heartbeat.

I'd never been mad at Matthew before. Not really. But I was suddenly furious, madder than I'd ever been at anyone. Ever.

"My grandpa says people who attack others for no reason are doing nothing more than pointing out their own character defects and personality flaws." My voice cracked.

He turned to me, eyes blazing. "Don't you ever have any thoughts of your own? I've had a bellyful of 'My grandpa says this' and 'My dad says that.' But you know what really gets me? The way you're always saying 'Do you know what Johanna told me?' or 'When Johanna and I were talking . . .' It's like you think she belongs to you or something."

I saw red. One moment I was just standing there and the next I was shoving Matthew backward so hard he fell flat on his back.

He scrambled up and socked me in the ear. I grunted from the pain and hit him back, then tackled him. We were rolling around on the ground, fists flying. Somehow I knew enough to roll away from the flower bed. I grabbed a fistful of his T-shirt and dragged him with me.

We snarled and punched and kicked. Dylan was barking like crazy and running around us, unsure whether we were playing or not. Matthew popped me on my cheekbone and I swung back as hard as I could and caught him on the left eye with a sound like a hammer hitting a melon.

We stopped fighting then, staring at each other, holding our sore eye and cheek, panting and confused.

"What's going on?" I asked him. "Why are we fighting? We never fight."

"It's . . . Johanna."

"What's Johanna?"

"I can't stop thinking about her."

"Oh," I said.

"Yeah, oh."

"I . . . uh . . . I feel the same way."

"Oh."

"Yeah, oh."

"There's . . . something . . . The way she throws her head back when you make her laugh." He looked over at her house.

"Or . . . when you're talking to her . . . and she leans in to listen harder . . ."

"No one's ever . . . talked to me like she does."

"No one's ever listened to me like she does."

"I love that. I . . . well, I guess, I kind of love . . .

her." He picked up the binder, which was next to his foot.

"Me too." I stopped, amazed. I'd had no idea I was going to say that. "Not like I feel about Karla, but . . ."

And there it was, I thought. Matthew and I had come to love Johanna. I'd never loved anyone but family before and I'm pretty sure Matthew hadn't either.

"I didn't know that until just now," he said.

"Me either."

We sat staring at the dirt, thinking. Johanna's laugh rang out from the front yard and we got up and walked around the house. She was leaning against her bike, just back from a training ride with a group of women. They hugged her and pedaled off, waving to us.

"Hello, garden boy. Hello, friend of garden boy. What's new?"

We looked at each other, knowing we had no intention of answering *that* question.

"How was your ride?" Matthew asked.

"Brutal."

"You swim tomorrow?"

"Yep. I'm on a one-sport-a-day training regime. I like the swimming part best. I'm not the best swimmer, but I float great. And, in the interest of full disclosure: I don't so much run as I walk briskly. Some days I even stroll."

"Johanna," I said, "how are you going to do the race? It's coming up really fast and you don't seem ready."

She bent down to the sidewalk. "A lucky penny. Let's all make a wish."

"I wish I could . . . uh, remember all the words to the songs on the radio," Matthew said.

"I wish you could too." Johanna and I spoke at the same time and then laughed.

"What do you really wish for, Johanna?" Matthew asked.

"I wish I could see the garden all done."

"That's not very excit—" I started to say, but then Matthew pegged me square in the solar plexus with the garden binder. I went over backward, the wind knocked out of me.

I sat on the ground, rubbing my chest. "That really hurt. What's your problem?"

He looked at me, shook his head and glanced at Johanna, who was rubbing noses with Dylan. Her eyes were bright. Bright like when she'd asked me to do the garden for her.

I didn't know exactly what had just happened, but I knew that a second thing we weren't going to talk about with Johanna had just occurred.

16

Every so often, Dylan would show up with a note clutched between his teeth, wagging his tail and wiggling all over like he'd just done a good trick or seen someone drop a pork chop.

I'd gotten three notes so far. Two were typed. One was scribbled by hand. They were all torn and spitty from Dylan's mouth, too smudgy in places to read clearly. He'd bring one to me and I'd read it, shove it into my pocket.

When I got undressed at night, I'd take the note from my pocket, smooth it out and put it in the wooden cigar box where I keep cool things, like the gold coin my grandpa gave me and the receipt from the ice cream place where Karla and I went on our date.

The fourth note, the one Dylan had brought me earlier today, read: *Family is who you find.*

They were like fortune cookies without the General Tso's chicken.

The first one made me wonder if Dylan had been going through someone's garbage, like when the spider and the pig sent that rat to the dump to find words the spider could write in her web in that book *Charlotte's Web*, and the rat would rip pieces of labels off boxes to bring back to the barnyard.

I was too tired from the garden to read my stack of novels for very long like I usually do at night. So I'd lie there in the dark and think about the notes.

Normally, I would have asked Matthew what he thought, but for some reason the notes were too private.

I kept them because I like words.

I kept them to myself because I knew they meant something special.

I kept thinking about them because I knew they were from Johanna.

17

 "Grandpa and Auntie Bean are contemplating living in sin."

"What did you just say?" Johanna stared.

"My grandfather and your Auntie Bean are thinking of renting an apartment and moving in together."

Johanna was just coming back from swimming. I was sitting on the curb in front of her house, waiting to talk to her.

"He's leaving the—"

"Assisted-living retirement community, yes. They came over for supper last night and told us."

"I'm glad they're happy."

"Hmmm."

"You have room for one more hungry mouth at your place?"

"Sure." I hesitated. "I asked Karla to come over and eat with us."

"You really like this girl, don't you?"

"Even more than I thought. I used to think she was perfect, but now that I know her, I see that she's better than perfect. She's . . . funny and smart, and even though she's so pretty it's hard to breathe, I, uh, I dunno. I like being with her."

"Were you scared when you called to ask her over tonight?"

"Terrified."

"Then you're doing it right. C'mon, let's eat; I built up a huge appetite in the pool today."

I started to lead her into the backyard, where I could hear Fernanda laughing with Dad as they set the picnic table. I looked over at Matthew and Karla sitting on the steps sharing a comic book he'd brought over. Grandpa and Auntie Bean were swinging together in the hammock.

"Hey, Johanna?"

"Hmmm?"

"Well, Dad and Fernanda are dating, and Grandpa and Auntie Bean are . . . whatever, and even I'm hanging out with Karla."

"Um-hmm."

"We're not a family of men anymore."

"No. Now you're just a family."

"How'd you do that?"

"How did Dylan come to live with you?" She seemed to be changing the subject.

"My dad found him on campus."

"He was a stray?"

"He didn't belong to anyone so Dad brought him home."

"That's kind of what my family does. Only, with people."

I stopped to think on what she was talking about as she continued into the backyard.

I heard Karla say, "Johanna, will you go school-clothes shopping with me in a few days?"

"First day is just around the corner, huh?"

"I'm kind of looking forward to school starting next week," I said as I sat down at the table.

"*You?*" Johanna and Matthew blurted.

"Yeah, well, right now all I do is worry about rabbits and weevils and the weather. School doesn't seem so bad. Weird, huh?"

"Only for you, Finn, only for you."

Everyone laughed and so did I. That was a first.

"Dude," Matthew said, "what's with all the rocks behind the garage?"

"They're from the yard. I picked them out of the ground."

"What are you going to do with them?"

"Hope that rock genies take them away in the night?"

"And what's with that"—he looked toward a corner of the yard—"gaping hole?"

"Dylan tried to help and dug a hole when I wasn't looking."

"Hmmm . . ." Matthew was thinking hard. "Got it! We can build a fire pit—you know, like an outdoor fireplace. We can line the hole with the rocks and dump in some of that leftover concrete from the stepping stone project."

"I'll get the binder and make the changes."

When I came back outside to the table with the gardening binder, Fernanda said, "Finn, have you lost weight?"

I stood a little straighter.

Then Auntie Bean said, "And you've gotten taller this summer, too."

I squared my shoulders, glanced at Karla to see if she agreed, and started to answer. And then I saw Matthew and Johanna choking back laughter and knew they'd put Auntie Bean and Fernanda up to teasing me.

"Go ahead, laugh; I think Fernanda and Auntie Bean have great taste in men."

Before then I'd never even been in on a joke. I'd certainly never been a part of one like that.

After we'd sat together for a couple of hours eating and talking and laughing, Dad and I got up to start doing the dishes. Grandpa and Auntie Bean said they'd drive Karla and Fernanda home, and Matthew walked Johanna over to her place.

Later Dad and I sat on the back steps together admiring the lanterns he'd helped me hang in the trees. The stench from the manure was just a distant memory, and in the dark it was easy to overlook the straggly flower beds and the sun-wilted vegetable patch.

"This is nice," Dad said. "You know, I didn't realize I was always at the library and never home. I like not rushing from work to class or study groups all the time. Sitting out here in the evenings with you is"—he draped an arm across my shoulders and looked around—"the best part of my day."

18

The night before the triathlon Johanna had a party.

When I saw all the food in the kitchen, I wondered if her family made hot dishes and dips on some sort of assembly line and then froze them in a huge walk-in freezer. They always seemed to have party food ready to go.

The house was loud and hot and crowded. I couldn't hear anything Matthew said because the music was so loud it was making my back teeth jiggle.

"Matthew, isn't this the best party you've ever been to?" I hollered in his ear.

"Finn, this is only the second party you've *ever* been to."

"And just think: all I wanted to do this summer was avoid people, and yet here I am."

"Yeah, talking to people just like you were normal or something."

I hadn't seen her come in, but all of a sudden Karla was next to me. She slipped her hand into mine. For a few seconds that thing where I couldn't think or breathe happened again. Only, in a good way, a really good way.

She'd brought some friends from school and I saw Matthew make this really smooth move where he cut Kari away from the pack and got her alone to talk to.

The music stopped abruptly and Johanna waved for everyone's attention. Someone had printed up dozens of pink TEAM JOHANNA—SWIM/BIKE/RUN FIND A CURE T-shirts so Johanna's cheering section would all match. Everyone pulled theirs on and it was like a bubble-gum factory had exploded in Johanna's house.

"Hey," Johanna called as we were all tugging shirts over our heads, "I want to thank everyone for, well, for . . ." I'd never seen Johanna run out of words. The room got quiet and Johanna's mom was suddenly real interested in straightening the food table and other people needed to get another glass of wine or piece of cheese.

"Does anyone have an ax?"

I dropped a huge hunk of Auntie Bean's cake. Dylan caught it on the way down, swallowed and looked for more.

"Or a chain saw? A chain saw might be better." Some big guy was speaking.

"Chuckie," Johanna said, "what do you need an ax and a chain saw for?"

"Those bushes?" He pointed out her side window to the lilac bushes that separate our yards. "Did you know there's a garden on the other side? I could trim the bushes and then I bet you could see those roses from your bedroom window."

"They're not my bushes and we have to leave them where they are."

"They're *my* bushes," I said, finding my voice. "If Chuckie hacks away at them from *our* side, then, really, that will be okay."

I would have said anything at that point. Someone wanted to look at my garden. Someone thought *my garden* was worth hacking down a bunch of lilacs to see. I'd have let him burn down my house.

"I have an ax in the garage," Dad said.

"Lead the way." Chuckie was rubbing his hands together as he followed Dad outside. A few minutes later Chuckie had cut about four feet of lilac bush down to nubbins.

And Johanna could see the rosebushes from her bedroom.

Later, I was taking about the twenty-eighth bag of garbage to the curb when Johanna motioned to me. She and Matthew were standing in the space where the lilac bushes had been, and I had to admit: Chuckie had done a really nice job.

She held two wrapped packages in her hands.

"I wanted to get you something to thank you for being such a help with the fund-raising this summer."

We ripped the paper off and saw that she had gotten us each a notebook exactly like the one she'd asked us to sign on the day we met.

"I know you don't keep journals, but I hope you at least take time every day to write down the best thing that happened to you."

She pulled us into a tight hug and I knew that even though it would probably be the only word we did write, Matthew and I would definitely put her name in our books.

19

 That was probably one of the greatest days of my life.

That night, however, was probably the worst night of my life.

Everyone had left by midnight, wanting to be at the race start by seven the next morning. Matthew and I were too amped on sugar to sleep so we stayed to clean up.

We were washing the dishes when we heard Dylan yip from the hallway.

We found him pacing outside the bathroom. When he saw us, he put his shoulder against the closed door and tried to shove it open. We could hear Johanna being sick.

Matthew rapped on the door. "Hey—how ya doin' in there?" She didn't answer. We stood looking at each other. Dylan whined.

Finally, Johanna opened the door. She looked gray. Her hands were shaking.

"I trained so hard," she said. "I pushed to get ready for the race tomorrow, but . . . Don't . . . don't call my mother; I don't want to make a fuss. I had chemo a few days ago, I knew the timing was wrong, but I hoped . . . Can you . . . would you stay awhile?"

Matthew and I led her to her room and helped her get into bed. Dylan curled up next to her.

None of us said anything. There wasn't anything to say.

We tucked her in and she fell asleep. But she tossed and turned and called out.

I was watching her and I said to Matthew, "Even though we probably should, I'm not going to call her mother. Or my father."

"We can handle it." Matthew's voice was thick.

I glanced over at him and was shocked to see tears in his eyes.

And then it hit me.

Hit me for the very first time. Hit me like the grenade that cancer is.

Oh, my god, I thought, Johanna is sick.

Really sick.

Until that very minute, her cancer had never felt . . . real. Had never been threatening.

We'd never talked about it. Not really. All those hours together working in the garden and making the stepping stones and hanging out here in her house, she'd never once complained. She'd never acted scared or angry.

And so it had never occurred to me that Johanna wouldn't get better.

I'd honestly believed that it was only a matter of time until the chemo worked and she didn't need the wig she always wore and she gained some weight. Lots of people beat cancer. It happens all the time.

It had never once crossed my mind that she might not see the garden, our garden, her garden, when it was finished.

But Matthew had known. That was why he'd dropped the plate, why he'd thrown the binder at me when I started to tease Johanna about her wish on the lucky penny.

I was freezing cold to my bones and yet numb all over. My mouth tasted like copper—the taste of fear. I felt like I might throw up, too, and my eyes stung so bad I could hardly see.

How could I have been so surprised and why hadn't Matthew told me? Because, I could see, looking at his face across her bed, this information was new only to me.

"You okay?" he asked.

"No. Are you?"

"Not even a little bit."

I was all of a sudden so tired that when I looked at

the bed, there were two Johannas and only half a Dylan.

I thought morning would never come.

Finally, around five, Matthew yawned and mumbled, "We need coffee. Go make coffee."

"I didn't know you drank coffee."

"No time like the present to start. My mother comes downstairs every morning saying something about feeling like the walking dead. She has a couple cups and she starts to act like herself again."

I puttered around in the kitchen, throwing in a couple extra scoops. We'd need the extra buzz. When the coffee was done, I put the pot, two mugs and spoons, milk and sugar on a tray.

In Johanna's room, Matthew and I poured enough milk into our cups to make the coffee a light brown and dumped in sugar. I tasted it.

"This is awful."

"Don't talk. Just drink. My mother doesn't start to make sense until midway through her third cup."

"Three might kill me."

"*I'll* kill you if you don't let me drink my coffee in peace."

"Are you always so crabby in the morning, Matthew?" Johanna's voice surprised us.

We looked over at her.

"Were you guys here all night?"

It's still night, I thought. "No big deal," I said.

"How do you feel?" Matthew asked.

"How do I look?"

Like roadkill, I thought. "Like you could use a little more rest," I said.

"I'm not the only one."

We stared out the window and watched the sky turn from black to purple and then to orange and pink.

Even though he'd had two cups of coffee, Matthew fell asleep just as the sun came up. That was when we found out that he could sleep sitting up and, I swear, with his eyes open.

I felt jittery and buzzy and wide awake. I looked over and saw that Johanna was watching me.

"I don't know how to thank you," she whispered.

"You don't have to." I moved closer so our conversation wouldn't wake Matthew.

"Weird way to spend your summer vacation."

I thought for a minute. "In a way, it's the least weird thing I've ever done." She bit her lip, listening to me. "I know that's a funny thing to say, but it . . . it was really . . . nice . . . to . . . to be . . ."

"Needed."

"Yeah. You know what I mean, then?"

"Yeah, Finn, I know what you mean."

"Okay."

"Yeah, okay."

"But, Johanna?"

"Yeah?"

"I am a terrible, awful, horrible gardener."

She smiled.

"Johanna?"

"Yeah?"

"Matthew and I will compete in your place in the triathlon today; we want to be your proxies instead of the friends you set up. Matthew will swim and run. I'll bike. Slowly."

She closed her eyes and leaned her head back against her pillow. "Finn, I've been waiting for someone like you my whole life."

20

 As soon as Johanna's folks arrived, we told them about her rough night. They tried to talk her out of even going to the race, but Johanna said, "I wouldn't miss this for anything. I'll even sit in the damn wheelchair, but I am going."

Pat and Dick exchanged a look over her head and agreed.

Matthew and I were halfway out the door on the way to register when she called, "Hey!"

We turned.

"I wanted to wait to tell you on the day of the race: Team Johanna raised eleven thousand, one hundred and sixty dollars and thirty-eight cents."

It was the sun in my face that made my eyes water.

While Matthew grabbed his running shoes and swim trunks, I dashed over to my house to tell Dad that

Matthew and I were filling in for Johanna. We jumped on our bikes and zipped over to Centennial Beach.

The crowd was huge—thousands. I'd had no idea so many people would show up. Nearly everyone in the park had pink ribbons pinned to their shirts or painted on their cheeks. I was glad we were wearing our Team Johanna shirts.

We checked in and were inked on our thighs and upper arms and calves with Johanna's entry number. As a volunteer pinned the numbered bibs to our backs, she said, "You've got white bibs; the pink bibs signify a survivor. You know this is a super-sprint triathlon, right? The swim portion is a quarter-mile, the biking is six point two miles, and the last leg, running, is one and a half miles."

"Piece of cake," Matthew said. Another volunteer led him over to line up for the swimming. I didn't have a chance to tell him I wasn't so sure I had 6.2 miles in me. I wasn't much of a bike rider and I'd never been in a race, much less a race in front of a crowd like this.

Before I could panic, another volunteer led me and my bike over to the transition area. Matthew would finish the swim and then would jog over from the beach and tag me so I could ride onto the course. When I got back to the bike racks, I'd tag Matthew so he could set off on the last part of the race.

I was starting to worry—about the heat, Johanna, Matthew finding me, following the route. Then I heard someone yell, *"Finn!"*

I looked up and saw Dad holding Dylan's leash. Karla was next to them. So was Matthew's dad. Grandpa had Fernanda and Auntie Bean on either arm. Dylan was wearing a sandwich board, and pink ribbons had been tied to his collar. One side of his sign read: WE LOVE YOU, FINN. WOOF. Dad had Dylan move so that I could see the other side: WE LOVE YOU, MATTHEW. WOOF. I smiled and waved as my stomach settled down. They turned and made their way to the start line to root for Matthew.

I couldn't spot Johanna in the crowd. Had she been able to make it?

Then came the air horn blast, a roar from the crowd and a distant splash as the swimmers hit the water in a wave of bodies.

Someone grabbed my hand. Johanna. Pat and Dick were standing behind her with the wheelchair, which had pink ribbons wound through the spokes of its wheels. Johanna squeezed my hand and then they slipped into the crowd.

I looked down. Johanna had handed me a note: *Don't question the miracles; they just might stop coming.*

It felt like only seconds later when the dripping swimmers started running past me to the bikes. I jumped up and down, searching for Matthew. Then he was shaking his wet head all over me and laughing, "That was amazing." He slapped my shoulder, making the handoff official. "Go! See you in six miles."

I jumped on my bike and tore out of the lot. At first

everything was a blur—I just saw colors in the crowd along the street and heard one big solid cheer. The bike wobbled underneath me and my legs were like jelly. My hands were numb; my heart was thumping. How would I follow the traffic cones and make the tight turns that got us out of the downtown area and into the neighborhoods? My back wheel skidded around one turn and I almost lost my balance. The scare cleared my mind, though, and I felt a sudden rush from my head to my toes.

I started to settle down and everything became distinct. I saw smiling, laughing, screaming faces in the crowd and heard voices calling out, things like "Looking good, Number Seventy-five!" "Way to go, Lisa!" and, more times than I could count, "Thank you . . . thank you . . . thank you!"

The air, which had been sticky and thick earlier, was suddenly fresh and clean on my face. The coppery taste of fear that had been heavy on my tongue since the night before had disappeared. I didn't even feel my legs pumping. For a few minutes, I thought the scenery was flying past me while I stayed still.

People stood in front of their houses, spraying us down with their hoses, dashing out to hand cups of water or open bottles to us as we rode by, holding up signs that read YOU CAN DO IT and YOU'RE ALMOST THERE.

Matthew had been right: this was amazing.

I felt so strong, like I could have biked forever. I started waving back at the crowd and found myself in the middle of a group of bikers all riding at the same pace. We were pedaling in unison, part of a slick, well-oiled machine.

I saw the finish line coming toward me way too soon.

I was focusing on following the guy in front of me through the last block of the race when I heard, "Finn!" Matthew was balancing on the top rail of the bike racks, yelling and waving both arms. I put some extra punch in my legs and came screaming up to him, making a horrible squealing sound with the brakes, fist-bumping him hard before he flew out of the transition area toward the running start line.

I dropped my bike and helmet and leapt over the racks so I'd get to the street in time to see Matthew rounding the corner. We flashed each other a thumbs-up. I started making my way through the crowd to the finish line and caught sight of Johanna, sitting in the shade.

I ran over, picked her up in my arms and spun her around. "Did you see me? Did you see Matthew? He looked great. I don't even know our times. Johanna, you should have seen the people on the bike route."

She laughed and then pointed to the finish line as the crowd surrounding us started cheering. The first three pink-bibbed survivors neared the finish line.

They slowed down, linked arms and high-kicked together past the clock, which marked them all as finishing at the same moment. Then they turned to wait for the rest of the runners in pink bibs to join them, hugging and high-fiving each other.

And then we saw Matthew, breathing hard and dripping as he gave one last kick and flew across the finish line. As soon as he spotted Johanna, he ran over and swooped her up like I had, laughing.

He put her down, then turned to me and thumped my back so hard I coughed.

"We did it!"

21

 After we collected our medals and had about a thousand pictures taken, a big group headed back to Johanna's house.

People ordered pizzas and Chinese food and my dad brought over zucchini bread and zucchini lasagna and zucchini meat loaf that he and Fernanda had made. Nothing else in the garden seemed to be thriving, but the zucchini patch was going crazy.

"The party," he told me under his breath, "is the perfect opportunity to unload some of this stuff."

The delivery guy from the liquor store showed up with a keg. We invited him to stay and soon he was helping set up the grill.

The party spilled from Johanna's house into her yard and over to ours. The more people who were in our yard, the better it looked.

Toward evening we were sitting around, Matthew and Johanna and I, talking about the race and the huge crowds. The party had been going on for hours—no one seemed eager to leave. Folks were sitting around playing cards and board games and some were even napping. Johanna seemed to have gotten some color back in her cheeks from all the company.

"Good thing I couldn't do the race. I wouldn't be caught dead in a swimsuit in broad daylight in front of that many people," Johanna said.

Matthew shot me a look and jerked his head for me to follow him. "I have an idea," he said. He whispered to me for a few minutes and I nodded, grinning.

"Excuse me!" I jumped up on the picnic table and dinged a spoon on a glass to get everyone's attention. "Nobody leave until we get back. We've got a surprise and we'll need about an hour before we can tell you what it is."

While I was talking, Matthew pulled my dad and Fernanda aside. Matthew and Dad were going to run to the hardware store while Fernanda drove me to Matthew's grandmother's house and the mall and then to meet him at the beach.

An hour later, as it was getting dark, we came back to the party and I dinged a glass with a spoon again. "We're back. Follow us now, but no questions or you'll ruin our surprise."

Everyone followed Matthew onto the sidewalk,

where he whispered to Dick, who smiled and nodded and took Johanna by the arm to his car. Dylan jumped into the backseat. The rest of us kept walking behind Matthew, like a parade without floats. Finally, after we'd been walking for about ten minutes, he stopped, looked at me and nodded. I waited until Dick and Johanna got to us from where they'd parked the car. Then I cleared my throat.

"We're coming up to Centennial Beach, and I have to ask all the cowards to leave us now."

Matthew continued, "Because we're about to break the law. Vandalism, I think, as well as unlawful entry, and if we're lucky, some of you will commit public indecency."

"What do you have planned here, boys?" Johanna looked excited.

"Skinny-dipping, now that the sun has gone down and the beach is closed. We cut the lock on the far gate so we can sneak in, and this way"—I paused— "*everyone* can be in the water because it's not in public or in broad daylight."

Everyone laughed and we followed Matthew down the path and around the back fence to the far gate.

He'd bought a bolt cutter at the hardware store and snipped the lock, but he'd set a new lock on the ground to replace the ruined one.

We snuck through the fence and everyone looked down the hill to the lake. I'd set up candles in glass jars along the steps and at the water's edge and their reflections flickered in the water. Piles of towels sat on a picnic table.

"Matthew's grandmother doesn't have a single canning jar left, or a single towel, and I hope she won't be mad at us for taking them," I said. "And the candle shop at the mall has been wiped out. But this seemed like a good cause."

Johanna stared at the water for a long time before she turned to us. "Let's go!"

"Nope." Matthew and I shook our heads. He said, "Finn and I are going to stand guard here at the gate. We'll whistle or scream or something if the cops come . . . give you time to get some clothes on before you're arrested."

We stood looking at each other, Johanna, Matthew and I, while everyone else went down to the water and dove in. Some stripped down to their birthday suits, some plunged in fully clothed.

Johanna smiled at Matthew, *just* at him, and then at me, *just* at me. Then she joined the others in the water.

We leaned against the fence and listened to them splash and laugh in the dark.

Although we were supposed to be keeping our eyes on the other side of the fence, the light from the candles flickered images at us. In the soft yellow-gray glow, we saw flashes of skin.

Grandpa and Auntie Bean shared an inner tube as they floated in the shallow end of the lake.

My dad held Fernanda's hand while they talked, sitting in the sand by the water's edge.

Dylan paddled over to the floating dock and someone hoisted him up. He shook the water from his coat, making everyone on the dock scream.

I didn't look, even though I wanted to, but I saw Matthew turn his head when we heard Karla and Kari laugh as they jumped in at the deep end. He grinned when I caught his eye, and his voice cracked when he spoke. "Amazing . . . just . . . amazing."

And before it was all over, we saw just one more thing: a man dancing with his wife at the water's edge to music only they could hear. He put a hand where her right breast had been as he bent to kiss her.

Johanna was behind us at that moment, bundled in a huge sweatshirt. She slipped between me and Matthew, putting her arms around us and pulling us tight. "Cancer can't ever touch that."

It was the first time Johanna had told me something I already knew.

EPILOGUE

Although I never did ask Johanna about the notes, I know she gave them to Dylan to deliver to me. I try not to wonder what she saw in me, sitting on the front steps with a book, that made her know there were so many things I needed to hear. But I hope she knew how much it meant to me to hear them.

On the day we first met, I asked her if she was named for Johanna from the Bob Dylan song; she didn't answer and I never thought to ask her again. But I always remembered, and late one night years after that summer we spent together, I finally looked up the lyrics and the last line hit me: "And these visions of Johanna are now all that remain."

My dad would kill me if I said this to him, but Bob Dylan had it wrong.

I had five notes in a small wooden box.

I had a stepmother and a stepgrandmother and a girlfriend.

And I had my garden.

Those are what remained from my summer with Johanna. Not visions at all.

For information about cancer, specifically breast cancer, and how women and their families deal with it, explore these Web sites:

www.komen.org
www.cancer.org
www.thebreastcancersite.com
www.breastcancer.org
www.nationalbreastcancer.org
www.cancer.gov/cancertopics

ABOUT THE AUTHOR

Gary Paulsen is the distinguished author of many critically acclaimed books for young people, including three Newbery Honor books: *The Winter Room*, *Hatchet*, and *Dogsong*. His novel *The Haymeadow* received the Western Writers of America Golden Spur Award. Among his Random House books are *Lawn Boy*; *The Legend of Bass Reeves*; *The Amazing Life of Birds*; *The Time Hackers*; *Molly McGinty Has a Really Good Day*; *The Quilt* (a companion to *Alida's Song* and *The Cookcamp*); *How Angel Peterson Got His Name*; *Guts: The True Stories Behind* Hatchet *and the Brian Books*; *The Beet Fields*; *Soldier's Heart*; *Brian's Return*, *Brian's Winter*, and *Brian's Hunt* (companions to *Hatchet*); *Father Water, Mother Woods*; and five books about Francis Tucket's adventures in the Old West. Gary Paulsen has also published fiction and nonfiction for adults, as well as picture books illustrated by his wife, the painter Ruth Wright Paulsen. Their most recent book is *Canoe Days*. The Paulsens live in Alaska and New Mexico and on the Pacific Ocean.

You can visit the author at www.garypaulsen.com.